Redneck Goddess

To my fellowwriter
& friend Joyce,
Enjoy the read &
let me know what
you think.
Pamela Foster

Redneck Goddess

Pamela Foster

HHP

High Press, USA Hill

Published by High Hill Press, Missouri
No part of this publication may be reproduced in any form without the prior written permission of the author. The book in its entirety may not be reproduced without written permission of High Hill Press.

HighHillPress@aol.com
www.highhillpress.com

First High Hill edition:
10 9 8 7 6 5 4 3 2 1

Cover Art by Joyce Craig
Cover Design by High Hill Art Department
ISBN: 978-1-60653-044-3
Library of Congress Number in publication data.

To my mom, who told me, "Honey, you can tell the truth or you can make it interesting.

Thank you, first of all, to my husband for his support and for his ability to ignore, on a fairly regular basis, the ranting of a writer.

I owe a huge debt to the Northwest Arkansas Writer's Group. Velda Brotherton and Dusty Richards are first class mentors. Clair Croxton and Jan Morrill gave unstintingly of their time and computer expertise. Ruth Burkett Weeks paved the way and, even more importantly, laughed the loudest at my readings. Duke Pennell and Gregg Camp never lost patience, at least not in my hearing, with my inability to properly use a comma or distinguish between a dash and a hyphen.

PROLOGUE

How a good ole girl from Noisy Creek Georgia ended up with a gorgeous Latin from The Republic of Panama is still a mystery to most of my kinfolk. Hell, some days even I can't sort through the twists and turns, bad choices, and undeserved blessings that brought me here. Of course, a good many of my family would have you believe the joining of a redneck goddess and a dark skinned foreigner is a good bit closer to curse than it is to blessing.

Well, times they are a changing but it does take a mighty powerful push to get the wheels moving and the engine of progress engaged in rural Georgia.

To paint you a picture here, think of my home town as a fine looking, hard working mule that has plowed the same field all his life. This here mule knows every rock and each spot of sandy soil in his domain, can predict an afternoon shower when dawn is still a fine golden promise on the horizon. This son of a jackass is right where he belongs. He knows his place in the world. Now, just for the sake of illustration, let us introduce into the life of this fine ass, a great green Harvester tractor with all the disk harrows and plough blades invented in the last fifty years by men intent on forcing the earth to yield up a crop.

I believe you can see that, while that growling tractor may be progress, that ole mule ain't gonna take to it kindly.

Now I myself love this ole mule of a town and pretty near every blessed soul that abides here. Nevertheless, this is the story of how I rode into town, metaphorically speaking, on the biggest shiniest tractor ever seen there abouts and helped to penetrate the rich dark opinions of that insulated world deeper than it had ever been plowed before.

Love, you see, is the biggest, grandest, most destructive instrument of change on God's good earth.

Chapter One ★

Oil and water, hog jowls and caviar, Julio Hernandez Monterey and my hometown of Noisy Creek, Georgia—these are a few of the things that do not mix.

My grant to study the Brush Foot Moths of Panama ended two weeks ago. It's time to take my homesick self back to Noisy Creek and get on with the rest of my life. Unfortunately I have managed to complicate that journey considerably by leaping into bed with a gorgeous man.

Sweaty and spent, Julio's whisper tickles my ear, begins a low purr in my belly.

"Perhaps I go with you. Back to your beloved town."

His voice is filled with the confidence that he is bestowing on me a great honor—a desire to meet my family, take this thing we have going on to the next logical level. He's told me he loves me. I've grown almost comfortable with that hazy word of hope and fear. But the idea of him coming with me to Georgia, entering into my territory, meeting my family, this seems to me a far greater commitment, a surprising desire for intimacy that causes me to leap away from him on the rumbled sheets.

"Go with me?"

"*Si*! *Por que* no?" he asks reasonably enough.

"You have met my family, *mi carita*. You are, how you say, an orphan, no? But one happy family of tios and tias, this you have, yes? These I will now meet."

"I don't think your mother refusing to talk directly to me for six months after walking in on me naked in front of the open door to your refrigerator constitutes meeting your family."

"You would like to spend more time with my beloved mother?"

My answer to that is lightning quick. His sister, Dulce, has already informed me that his mother calls me The Flame Haired Whore. Though Dulce swears the name sounds much better in Spanish. I am not especially offended by this as I have a pretty good idea of the names my family might well invent if I show up in Noisy Creek with Julio. In Georgia my Latin Lover Extrordinare will be seen by at least a few of my relatives as, to employ a polite euphemism, a person of color.

Why oh why do these crucial conversations always seem to take place when the majority of my blood is still struggling to make its way up from my hinder regions. What I want, as my Auntie Ruth would say, is to have my cake and eat it too, but at the moment I can think of no way to have both Julio and Noisy Creek. My mind races through the facts and runs dead into that ole brick wall of bigotry.

In The Republic of Panama Julio is a mover and a shaker, a member of one of the dozen or so families who, basically, own the country. I know as a natural fact, none of that, is going to make a hill of beans difference in how my kin see him. All the money and education on God's good earth is just not going to prevent some of my blood kin from judging him based solely on the color of his skin and the country of his origin. In exactly the same way that his mama and a few of his family judge me based on the same criteria.

Julio, unaware of the direction my mind has taken, raises up on one elbow, nuzzles the hollow of my throat.

"We will go together to see your family. I will eat the meat of the alligator and do a hunt for the raccoon animal with your Uncle Earl, no?"

This idea of his to mingle with my family produces in my struggling brain a vision of a skiff overturning on a darkened lake, a hungry alligator undulating lazily through the tannic brown water. This mental flash is followed by an image of Julio strolling unsuspecting through piney woods with my Uncle Walter and his trusty hunting rifle directly behind him.

"Really? You want to go with me?"

My less than enthusiastic reaction seems to hurt his feelings. I roll back over on top of him, sit straddling his hips, look down at his lower lip protruding like that of an injured boy.

"Querido," I coo like a mother to a breastfed infant, "you know I care for you. But it is so different up north from the way it is down here."

"You are afraid your cracker family will call me greaser? Spick? What? You think I do not have the understanding that up there I am only another brown man?"

I cannot bear to look at his face, his dark eyes smoldering in anger and hurt, his jaw set firm, the angry tension in his neck and shoulders. I stretch myself along his length, kiss his stiff neck, murmur a half truth into his ear, "Sweetie, I just don't want you to be hurt."

He lifts me from him, cups my chin in his beautiful hand.

"I do not care what they think. For me, it matters only how I am in your eyes. This you decide. I have told you of my desire to go with you. Now you tell me and I either go or I stay."

He rises from the bed, all feline grace and dignity, leaving me alone on its king-sized expanse feeling small and mean.

That night we eat at Mi Ranchito on the causeway and enjoy the lights of the skyscrapers reflecting in the night waters of the bay on the right with The Bridge of the Americas stretching like a jeweled necklace over the dark waters of the canal on the left. I eat scallop filled corvina as though it is my last meal—slowly and savoring every bite. A half moon makes its way over the lights of the highrises packed along the curve of the bay. A lunar blessing falls on the smooth surface of the water, conjuring up in me an intense joy. The lighted ships sprinkled across the entrance to the canal, the bridge suspended over a freighter just now beginning its passage, the man sitting across me who keeps smiling into my eyes, all this I take as a benediction.

After supper Julio suggests a stroll along the causeway. I've slipped off my new yellow sandals and when I feel around under the table for them with my toes, one is hiding.

"You have removed your little shoes?" Julio asks as though this is just the cutest thing ever done by a woman and disregarding the pure fact that I have not worn little shoes since I was six. He adjusts his linen pant legs, squats beside me with his head nearly in my lap, and peers under the table to locate my missing size nine. The restaurant has become watchfully quiet, but I refuse to look up. Julio locates my sandal. He displays it to me like the world's sexiest shoe salesman, takes my bare foot in his hand, brings it to his bowed head and touches his warm mouth to my instep. He slips the sandal on my foot, stands effortlessly and bows from the waist to kiss me. The restaurant roars with applause.

In this moment I am stunned to admit that I am irrevocably in love with this man.

This realization nearly paralyzes me with fright. Loving Julio means bringing him home and into the big, sloppy, loving, parochial bosom of my kinfolk. This action may well cut me off from the love that has sustained me since the day I stood in the driving rain under a canvas canopy, breathing in the finality of raw red dirt being shoveled into a muddy hole in the ground.

The tropical night is a warm embrace as Julio stands behind me on the causeway, that narrow strip of land that divides the depth of the Pacific Ocean from the shallow bay of the city. When he wraps his arms around me, pulls me back so that I am resting against the length of his body, I ache to tell him of my fears, to explain the shaking of my hands and the stiffness in my back and shoulders. But how do I explain my cowardice, how do I tell him I do not know if I can live without the love of my family?

My fear makes me again that newly orphaned child standing in the rain with the scent of loss permeating every cell. My aunties and uncles did their best to shelter me. They pieced together a crazy quilt of love and acceptance, stitched it tight with the strength of their will and attention. These good people drew that blanket over me, tucked it in good at the corners. Even then I insisted on kicking off the cover in the dark of the night, waking cold and alone.

Right now the warm salty breeze rattles the palms over our heads and I am once again that frightened child waking scared in the Georgia night.

Julio turns me to him, brushes a strand of my unruly red hair from my face and with a kiss he seals our fate.

Chapter Two

Those simple words "meet my family" feel like the equivalent of Evil Knievil deciding to fly his motorcycle across the grand canyon, except my means of conveyance over the dark chasm is going to be, not a rocket powered motorbike, but love.

For the month it takes to make the arrangements to leave Panama and return home, I am a mess. Nightly I wake from dreams of my Uncle Walter's flannelled back disappearing into a light I cannot reach. I flail in the twisted sheets trying to get my leaden legs to catch this man whose quiet love and acceptance brought me into whatever grace I have managed to attain.

I know that Uncle was infamous as the family rascal before my daddy, his oldest brother, died. Three beers in, every one of my uncles has a tale or two to tell of a dark and brooding, downright dangerous Walter. I never saw that side of him. Not once. After Daddy died Uncle Walter went once a week, Aunt Ruth says in the beginning it was once a day, to meet in the basement of the Jesus Christ the Redeemer Church with a group he called Friends of Bill.

None of that mattered to me. Uncle Walter was my safe place. Always. I fear losing the sanctuary of his love, of crossing a line which I will be unable to uncross. I know my night terrors are of disappointing him so much, that he will withdraw his love, but knowing their origin is no comfort.

Finally Julio sits me down on his uncomfortable sleek sofa, captures my fluttering hands in both of his and says simply, "I love you Georgia Ginny Barr. No worry, I promise, all will be well."

Since realizing that I have, as the song says, fooled around and fell in love, I am daily swamped with the strength of my feelings for this man. Occasionally I feel a little like I'm drowning in a warm salty ocean of life and love, but I am slowly learning to lean back, relax and let the density of the medium support me. That I'm currently accomplishing this relaxation for about three minutes a day is beginning to wear on both me and Julio.

"Why Goo Goo Barr! What on earth could you be thinking?" Aunt Ruth drawls when I tell her we will rent a car and drive on down to Noisy Creek arriving Thursday for supper.

"Whatever in the world would your young man think of us, lettin' y'all rent one a them vee-hicles? Child we'll be there to hug your neck the very instant you step off that big ole plane!"

I had hoped to ease Julio into the encounter with my family. Looks like he's in for the immersion method. I planned for the four hour drive to be akin to wading out into the surf and getting his legs wet before diving in to actually hand feed the sharks. Lord have mercy on my quaking soul, Sweet Jesus alone knows how many of my kinfolk will be meeting that plane.

I make a stab at preparing Julio for Noisy Creek, but soon give it up.

"You're going to get grits for breakfast," I tell him as we watch the wild parrots nesting on his balcony and sip our cappuccinos, nibble warm croissants

"To this I am looking forward," he assures me smoothly. "The grit is the large rat animal that we call the zorro, yes? In your back of the woods, it is typical breakfast fare. This I know."

"You're thinking of an opossum and it's neck of the woods, but never mind. Just be your gorgeous self," I tell him, adding quickly, "and stick close to me at all times."

Aunt Ruth is the only kin to whom I reveal my fears for Julio's acceptance into my loving and bigoted family. She tells me nearly the exact thing that Julio told me. Except she's nowhere near as sweet about saying it.

"If you're proud of him," she says sharply as though my fears are a judgement on the family, which they are no such thing, "the family will grow to accept him."

Though she does admit into my silence, "maybe not everyone will roll out the southern hospitality right at first, but if you're sure you love this young man and if he treats you like the princess you are, folks will come 'round."

From the steel in her voice I understand the discussion is closed. In truth all outsiders have a rough go at first when they enter the Noisy Creek Nation. We don't cotton much to outsiders.

"Ya'll ain't from around he-ah?" being the equivalent of "Welcome" in my neck of the woods.

I can already feel myself changing gears, shifting into Noisy Creek mode. Julio says my accent is getting stronger. In bed I shatter his concentration when I whisper into his ear "Darlin', y'all make me hotter an slickern'a tin roof in a Georgia rain."

The moment is only salvaged by a rapid switch to my fall back Spanish phrase.

"No importa. Mas!   Mas, por favor!"

It is an amazement to me that our love making doesn't set off every car alarm in the city.

Afterward, I reveal a family idiosyncrasy.

"You know my last name is Barr, right?" He props himself up beside me, gives me one of his heart stopping smiles. "Ok. The thing is, a good many folks in my family are, well, a good many of us are named after candy."

He strokes my arm, raising goose flesh and letting me know that this is a breather we are taking here. The night is still young.

"This I do not understand," he says as his hand moves to my belly.

I'm trying to focus my attention enough to finish warning him of this particular Barr idiosyncrasy.

"My daddy was Alman Barr. I have uncles named Clark and Hershey and aunties named Candy, Snickers and Baby Ruth."

The bed shifts as Julio sits up beside me.

"You are, how you say, pulling my foot?   No?"

"Nope. I am not pulling your leg. I have cousins called Nougat and Sugar Baby. Aunt Ruth told me yesterday there is even a brand new helpless baby boy already stuck with the name Mr. Peanut."

Julio accepts this family eccentricity with his usual good grace. He runs his hand slowly from my chin to my belly button.

"And you," he murmurs as his mouth follows his hand, "what is your sweet candy name?"

"Goo Goo," I gasp, "Goo Goo Barr."

He raises his head, arches his left eyebrow in confusion.

"It's an old southern favorite," I tell him with my hands on the back of his head.

His reply is muffled

We fly out of Panama in a pearl gray dawn. The skyscrapers of Punta Pacifica, the long crescent of Balboa Avenue, the chunky cement antiquity of Casco Viejo flow past the squared porthole before the sleek Delta jet breaks through low cloud cover and begins its climb. Suddenly this feels like a final goodbye to the city. Which prompts yet another attack of melancholy. Julio squeezes my hand before bringing it to his mouth where he pries apart the death grip of my fingers, smoothes them flat before kissing my palm.

"No worry," he tells me. "You will see. By tonight, everything will be better than the fur of a toad."

My laughter offends him only a little and it brings me out of my funk and into the promise of our next adventure.

"I think you mean finer than frog's hair and I'm not worried."

Not exactly worried. Anxious. Nervous. Joyful at the prospect of seeing my aunts and uncles. Thrilled to be dropping back into the middle of Noisy Creek, though somehow my breathing is a little ragged thinking about all that love and support. What with worrying a knife knot in my belly, I got no sleep at all last night. Now, with the jet still climbing into the atmosphere, I lay my head on Julio's shoulder and conjure up an image of what I'm leaving behind—glimmering rain drops on tropical green as deep and varied as God's own gift of love.

Julio doesn't wake me until we're nearly the last people to depart the plane. He takes both carry-ons from the overhead. Still half asleep, I follow him down the aisle, through the exit ramp and into the Atlanta airport. I blink twice, grin up at Julio and we follow the signs to claim our luggage. The baggage actually worries me a little.

I have one backpack which holds all my clothing and toiletries. By all I mean everything I own in the world: a few pair of ratty jeans, a half dozen t-shirts, some cotton underwear, New Balance sneakers and a pair of hiking boots that weigh as much as everything else in the pack.

My sweet Latin Lover, on the other hand, has six Louis Vuitton bags. A going away gift from his sainted mother, these suitcases are leather with a confusing variety of straps and buckles and side and back and front and under compartments. Six full suitcases and there isn't a pair of jeans or a t-shirt in the mix. I fear for my man, I truly do.

At the luggage carousel I head for those rental carts. The ones that invariably get hung together so that you put in your dollar and then fight like a lunatic to untangle them from their mates. Julio looks stricken. He shakes his head slightly and strides across the baggage area in his tailored suit, speaks in smiles and slow hand movements to an airport official, and before the first bag is coming down the ramp, he is back with a Mexican porter wearing overalls and a name tag that reads Jesus Jose Garcia. I quickly learn that Jesus has been in the United States for ten years and in Georgia since last March.

Julio silently hands Jesus Jose our baggage claim checks. I know from past discussions that he is both appalled and amused by my chit chatting with the help as though we were equals. Since, as I've explained several times to my love, I actually do believe everyone equally worthy of respect and consideration, I ignore him and go on being me. I know we southerners have a reputation as slave holders and all that historical hoopla, but frankly not a soul in my family ever owned a plantation or a human being either. For pure separation of the classes, y'all can't get any stricter than Latin American aristocrats.

I have my arm slipped through Julio's in a move known to all wrestling fans as The Georgia Grip when I hear my Aunt Thelma's voice. We haven't yet passed the non-passenger section of the airport but we now have a clear view of my relatives waiting at the end of the aisle.

"Thar she is! Lord she has just gotten as skinny as a wormy dawg!"

This is followed close by my Uncle Walter's deep growling bass.

"Sweet Jesus! Who is that nigga with his hands on our girl?"

Aunt Ruth's firm voice almost succeeds in drowning out Uncle. Almost.

"Goo Goo, welcome home child!" she calls down the aisle.

"Who is this handsome man you've brought us?"

I can feel the tension in Julio's arm as we keep striding, as if eager to get where we are going, toward well over a dozen of my relatives. The word ambush jumps into my head and plants itself like a tiny mustard seed of anxiety. Uncle Walter and Aunt Ruth are front and center in the welcoming committee. I remind myself that not one of my uncles could possibly have gotten a gun past the terrorist inspired airport security.

Aunt Ruth is wearing a pale green linen suit with the skirt cut on the bias. Uncle Walter is in clean Wranglers and the cotton shirt I bought him for his sixty-fifth birthday, the one the near exact shade of green as his eyes. I promised myself I would not leave Julio's side while he met my family. I meant it too.

Seeing Uncle Walter there, looking just slightly older than the last time I saw him, I forget about Julio completely, drop my arm from his and run home. The next little while, I hug necks, submerge myself in Uncle Walter's Bay Rum and Winstons, Uncle Earl's Sunday go to meeting Old Spice and stale Jax beer, the lavender scent Aunt Enid buys in tiny pyramid shaped bottles down at Longstreet's pharmacy and Aunt Ruth's unique blend of musk and gardenia.

"Lord," I cry to Aunt Candy, "anyone watching all this crying and wailing and carrying on would think I've just returned from a decade of foreign war."

Which finally reminds me that someone IS watching. My love who has never met any of these people.

The man I promised to ease into my big noisy family. I extridite myself from Aunt Enid's fleshy arms and step outside the circle to Julio who is patiently watching this greeting. I see the tightness in his shoulders, the slight stiffness as he extends his hand to Uncle Walter, but I'm certain my family is seeing a supremely confident man.

Uncle Walter keeps his hands in the pockets of his jeans and Julio merely turns into me and whispers into my ear.

"No worry. I am happy to see you now in your natural habitat."

Aunt Snickers kisses his cheek, hugs my neck again and proclaims, "Honey, this here man is just the handsomest thang I have laid eyes on since Hector was a pup."

As I should have been able to predict, the women in my family are more taken with Julio than are the men. Aunt Enid tentatively offers him her hand. He turns it palm up and kisses her wrist with the slight head bow I've grown to expect from a well bred Latin man meeting a woman for the first time. This greeting, common closer to the equator, is completely new to my family. Auntie blushes, jerks her hand from his mouth as if burned. I notice two or three other aunties pushing forward though for their turn to meet this handsome dark-skinned man I've brought home.

The men react completely differently. I see them cut their eyes to one another, move slightly closer to their women. I keep that wrestling grip on Julio's arm. Uncle Walter spots the hapless Jesus Jose standing patiently beside the luggage cart.

"Did this here Greaser hijack your luggage?" he accuses, "They'll do it ever last time. No need to pay one a these foreign buggers to pack your bags when you got yourself a whole dang family a strong men to heft em for ya."

"Walter!" Aunt Ruth says in her school marm voice, the one that courts no objections. "Why don't you go on out and bring the van around front so's the porter can load all this beautiful luggage on into it."

Uncle opens his mouth to object, looks around at the other men to see what backup he might expect, glances back at Aunt Ruth and concedes defeat. From the downcast eyes and nervous shifting of work boots, I can tell that the whole mess of them were led in the Manners Prayer by Aunt Ruth before they ever were allowed to come on this excursion. Uncle Clark calls it the Sunday School Teacher's Tirade to the Behaviorally Challenged and it begins with "Lord Jesus, help us to remember that we are southern ladies and gentlemen and as such our behavior today reflects directly on your sweet name."

When a Noisy Creek Baptist grabs your hand, bows their head and proclaims, "Let us pray," well there ain't a whole lot you can do to escape the lecture that is guaranteed to follow. Instruction that comes directly from the Lord Jesus through good southern women folk has been pretty much ruling my part of the country for years. So Uncle Walter may be fired up and looking for a fight, he may believe he is called upon to rush into the self-started fray and let the truth that foreigners are out to steal this here country right out from under our noses be clearly and loudly proclaimed by one God fearing white man. He may believe all of that down to his very toenails, but right now he's going to do what he is told. Uncle goes away muttering, but nobody doubts the van will be waiting for us when we get to the pickup area.

Chapter Three

Despite my best efforts, in the confusion of arranging sixteen people and eight pieces of luggage into six different vehicles, in the mêlée, Julio and I get separated. I end up with Aunts Enid and Thelma in Aunt Ruth's Volvo and I have a nightmare vision of a long linen trousered leg disappearing into Uncle Earl's beater pickup—the one with the matching bumper stickers, the left instruction 'Honk if you love Jesus' and the right suggesting 'Honk if you're horny.'

When I object to these travel arrangements Aunt Ruth soothes, "Now Goo Goo, you know your Uncle Earl would never hurt anyone you love."

As I watch Uncle's variegated green and gray and primer truck pull away, its dichotomy of instructions finally disappearing, I remember this same uncle hanging my beloved Wilbur by his hind legs and slitting his throat before he could even squeal. Sliding into the backseat of Aunt Ruth's Volvo I mutter, "I loved that pig."

Aunt Ruth, who has ears like a fox and I don't mean furry and pointed, merely gives me a warning look in the rearview mirror as she pulls the car out into its place in the Convoy of Love. The lead vehicle, the kidnapper in his beat-up truck and Aunt Pauline and Uncle Marcus in drag position in their thirty foot RV, have CB's. Every loving soul has a cell phone. We haven't gone ten miles when the men folk have declared that their bellies are rubbing against their backbones and the decision is made to stop for brunch at The Cracker Barrel. I'm planning a hostage rescue.

Aunt Thelma is telling me about Aunt Ruth and Collin's wedding. This is an event I'll never be forgiven for missing but which was unavoidable as it took place the same week as the annual migration of the Brushfoot Moths, the study of which was the justification for my grant in Panama. Aunt Snickers sent pictures over the internet, so I know that Aunt Ruth wore a silk suit the color of vanilla touched whipped cream and that she pulled her shoulder length hair, once strawberry blonde now spinning expertly toward gold, up on top of her head in a fancy braided knot. From the pictures that Aunt Snickers sent, I'd have never guessed she was fifteen years older than her new husband. I knew of the age difference of course, because every living soul in Noisy Creek had written or phoned to let slip this tiny little fact, followed inevitably by the words, 'course it's no never mind to me how young the boy is.'

I remember now that there are a number of opening statements common in my free thinking family that make my teeth hurt and my feet want to run. 'It's no never mind to me' being at the top of the list. There are others. Every last one of which begins a conversation like a flashing red light in your rearview mirror.

"Well, I don't like to judge but . . ."

"Child I don't want to hurt your feelings none but..."

"Now I my own self do not have a fancy college ed-U-ca-tion, but to my way of thinking . . ."

And my personal favorite:

"Honey child, I would just ne-vah in million ye-ahs tell y'all how to live your life, but . . ."

How could I have forgotten all these charming colloquial expressions, which now that I am home, rush nonstop into my brain? And what in tarnation is being said in that dented truck up there driving point in this platoon of welcome.

Aunt Ruth is telling me about the new housing development going in out on rural route twelve. Preston Yates, Aunt Snickers' new paramour, has bought up over a thousand acres, the entire south side of the mountain. He plans a gated community with five thousand square foot log cabin style hunting lodges, hiking and horse trails, and an equestrian center.

"The fool would put in a damn golf course if he could find enough folks with one leg shorter than the other to play it," Aunt Enid grumbles at me from the front seat.

"Folks with that kind of money will want to live in Noisy Creek? On a mountain as steep as Martin's Ridge?" I ask.

My mind creates a fuzzy image of some city slicker in perfectly creased jeans playing checkers in Confederate Square or setting a trot line out at Blackjohn Lake. I shake my head to clear the vision.

"Well, that there is the deal," nods Aunt Thelma. "Mr. Fancy Man, or as your Aunt Ruth calls him The Great Satan, is putting in a whole community with a market where they can buy special rich folk grub. Why the man has petitioned to put in a U.S. post office in Yatesville. That there is what he's calling this here place.

Yatesville. As if the whole darn mountain ain't been Martin's Ridge for all these years."

It's part of Noisy Creek history that when D. L. Martin returned from the War of Northern Aggression after distinguishing himself at Chickamauga, he took his young wife, a Foster girl if I'm remembering the story correctly, and isolated himself up on the steepest mountain in these parts. No one in town ever saw him again. His wife or one of his twelve sons would be seen from time to time buying flour or a length of gingham, but D. L. was never spotted again. Over the years his sons and grandsons and great-grandsons have moved down the mountain and intermarried with the rest of us rednecks. My high school boyfriend Samuel is a proud descendant of ole D.L. There's a lover's lane about a mile up the mountain at the end of an abandoned logging road where all us kids went to neck and spoon and scare ourselves goose pimply with tales of the ghost of D.L. still wandering that mountain, still fighting Yankees.

"Preston Yates is changing the name from Martin's Ridge to Yatesville?" I ask now. It's just a name, I know that, but still, it strikes me as sacrilegious. I'm surprised at how deeply offended I am by this affront to local tradition.

Aunt Ruth slides into the fray now and recants ever having publically called the man The Great Satan. She reminds us that this gentleman is the chosen beau of her sister Snickers and that he may someday be a member of our wonderful and gracious Christian family. Aunt Enid grunts, Aunt Thelma growls and I grin like a front teat calf. It's good to be home. It seems good strategy, as the daughter returning home with the not-from-around-he'ah new boyfriend to support Aunt Snickers.

"Well," I say. "I'm sure Mr. Yates must have some good qualities. You know," I add as I squeeze Auntie Ruth's hand, "or else why would Aunt Snickers be spending time with the man?"

For this attempt at diplomacy, I get an approving head nod from Aunt Ruth and another grunt from Aunt Thelma. Uncle Neil is calling on Aunt Ruth's cell phone with a topic more important than anything we might be discussing among ourselves. Auntie hands the phone to me.

"When we get to the restaurant," he instructs me solemnly as Aunt Ruth follows the rear end of Uncle Walter's jeep into The Cracker Barrel parking lot. "We want to get separate checks. I'll pay for the folks in your car, and for your . . . person," he stumbles but recovers almost smoothly building to the important point of these marching orders. "There is no way in heck I'm gonna pay for your Uncle Earl's meal."

We all know this on-going argument. In 1985 the Uncles Earl and Neil traveled to Bull Shoals Arkansas for a Bass fishing contest. Uncle Earl paid for their shared hotel room and their tournament entrance fees and Uncle Neil paid for all the meals. All us Barrs are tall and there isn't a one of us whose a pickey eater, but Uncle Earl is the tallest and the heaviest and the hands down best at chowing down. According to Uncle Neil, the man outdid himself in the grinds department on that trip. He also won the tournament with a Bass almost twice as big as the one Uncle Neil pulled into the boat. Then, on the ride home, he gloated that he hadn't paid a penny for the hotel room or the entrance fees. He won the whole darn deal in one of those fishing magazine contests he was always entering.

As we make our way across the parking lot of the Cracker Barrel and into the shade of the long front porch which is set up with a regiment of rocking chairs, all of us women have our walking papers. Separate checks. None of us want to listen to Uncle rehash that two decade's old fishing trip via cell phone for the five hours it's going to take us to get home.

Uncle Earl's truck is already parked and I walk fast across the lot, planning the ambush to recover my man. A melody I never in a million years thought I'd hear floats across the softened asphalt in the heavy Georgia air. Uncle Earl's gruff bass guffaws are mingling with Julio's smooth baritone laughter. I can see Uncle, one strap of his Dickie overalls hanging from his shoulder, his Brave's cap cocked slightly off-center on his big head. He has one foot propped on the back bumper of his old truck and he waves his arms in the air for punctuation. Julio stands with his legs spread slightly, his head tipped back, his laughter spilling up toward a cloudless, pale-blue sky.

"Your uncle, he is telling me of the time he catched a, how you say? Catfish? As big as a car and a alligator too. Same day. He is saying to me that he did this naked like a Day Bird."

"Jay bird," I correct automatically as I take his hand. I want to feel him all over to assure myself he is still in one piece, not damaged in any way. But these two are in the middle of man stuff. My concern will not be appreciated by Julio and it will grievously offend Uncle Earl. I keep my mouth shut and listen to Julio regale Uncle with a story of deep sea fishing for Marlin. I try to picture Uncle Earl on the sleek yacht that is shared by Julio's entire family. The boat is all polished teak and gleaming brass, long elegant lines and dual inboards. It's not that big a stretch really. Something that floats on the water, a fishing pole and a cooler of beer. These two may have discovered the universal language.

My relatives are shocked to discover that Julio has never been inside a Cracker Barrel. When told that Panama does not have this restaurant franchise, Aunt Enid seems stuck on the phrase, 'Why I just never even imagined such a thang' as though we've told her they don't have trees in that country, or air. While a contingent of uncles arrange for enough tables to be smooched together so that sixteen people, five of whom weigh over three hundred pounds, can sit together comfortably with enough room on the table for the abundance of food we are going to be ordering, we women, escorted by Julio and Uncle Earl, wander through the froufrou of items for sale in the vestibule store.

In the candy section, we all stand dumbly, struck back into our childhoods, staring at the jawbreakers and soft licorice and Sugar Daddys. Aunt Pauline insists on buying me a box of Goo Goo bars.

Over my weak objection she declares, "You cain't get these anywhere else now, don't ya know? Goo Goo you let me buy these here for you else wise I'll have to cook up a batch and in this heat that's just more than I can summon the strength to do."

In a section of nostalgic television paraphernalia, I listen to Uncle Earl unsuccessfully explain to Julio about Barney Fife and Andy and Aunt Bee and Opie. Uncle gives up and buys a CD of The Andy Griffin Show. I have an image of the two of them curled up in their jammies sharing a bowl of buttered popcorn and watching Aunt Bee fuss over Opie while Andy fens off his deputies requests for a bullet to go with his side arm. Julio pries my fingers from his arm where I have inadvertently left marks. He has taken off his suit jacket and rolled up his shirt sleeves.

He leans down and presses his mouth to my ear sending a shiver of goose flesh near down to my toes. "Your big happy family I like very much," he tells me.

Ah huh, just what that woman off the coast of South Africa was probably thinking as she hand fed the great whites. Right before she ran out of fish bait.

Seating arrangements are handled deftly by Aunts Ruth and Snickers, Uncle Walter theoretically neutralized by being seated between the two. The family is in agreement that Julio must try turnip greens and cornbread, black-eyed peas and collards, fried okra and buttermilk biscuits and chicken fried steak. There are the usual ten conversations going at once so that I hear only snippets from around the table.

"I like them green beans but since I had me that gallbladder flare up, they don't like me no mo . . .."

"I just am not that all fired hungry. Maybe just this here half a fried chicken and . . ."

"Don't know what she can be thinking, bringin' . . ."

"Pastor Coleman talked on that very thang two weeks past."

We have increased the noise in the room to what I call Barr Level. Other diners retaliate by raising their own voices in self-defense, and within two minutes the din is loud enough to stun a hog.

Over all this though, Uncle Walter manages to be heard as he calls down the full length of the co-joined tables, "What I'd like to know," his deep voice bellows into the cacophony, "is just how someone like you met up with our girl down there in that there place y'all are from."

The question I hear is, "Why would you think you are entitled to lay your hands on a white woman?"

If Julio understands the sub context, he gives no sign. He smiles pleasantly into the silence that has descended over the table like a shroud and explains how he met me at the opening of an art gallery in Casco Viejo. Julio was, of course, with one of his Latin Barbies, but he caught my eye across the room, strolled to me, bestowed upon me the Latin head bow and wrist kiss. He stood beside me silently then for what felt like a couple of lifetimes while we pretended to study the artist's work in front of us.

Finally he turned toward me, lifted a flame of my hair away from my ear, bent slightly and whispered, "I am, how you say, smitten. You are a most beautiful woman. May I call you, senorita?"

When I attempted to give him my number, he smiled, shook his head and told me there was no need, he would find me. I had no idea that I had just been invited to join the life styles of the rich and famous. Well, famous in the tiny Republic of Panama anyway. On Julio's end, he didn't have a clue that he had just met one of the few women in his country who looked upon his family's money and power more with suspicion and unease than with admiration. Months later he would tell me that he was as taken with my indifference to his wealth as he was to my fiery red hair and long legs.

To my Uncle Walter Julio says only, "I met your beautiful Georgia Ginny Barr at a gallery opening where there was hung the work of a new artist of my country."

Knowing southern men as I do, I wish he had used a different verb than 'hung,' but perhaps I'm not giving my Uncles the credit they deserve.

"Ah huh," Uncle Walter says in this maddening tone of voice as though Julio had said he broke into my house and spirited me away to ravage at will until my spirit was broken by his mighty dark-skinned well hung cock. "Well here's the deal son, we don't cotton none at all to persons of your particular color mixin' with our young white women."

Aunt Ruth has a hold of Uncle Walter's arm and is shaking it like a rag doll. Aunt Snickers has a look on her face I've only seen one other time and that was when my dog General Lee ate the Christmas turkey. I couldn't hurt more if Uncle had struck me with one of his ham sized fists. My body is straining to get up, walk the length of the table and punch my misguided uncle directly in his big fat nose.

But I've known something like this reception was inevitable since I stood on the causeway like Cinderella and invited Julio to come home with me. I push back my chair and make the walk to Uncle Walter, whose face now shows the realization that he may not have the backing he expected from the rest of the family. Plus, he can't possibly have any feeling in his arm with Aunt Ruth still shaking and squeezing while she combines this move with kicking his shin under the table. I walk directly into Uncle, squat beside his chair, put my arms around his thick neck and kiss his scratchy cheek.

"Uncle Walter," my voice cracks with tears as I whisper into his ear. "You've been there for me my whole life. I love you and I know you have my best interests at heart. You're entitled to your own views about how the world ought to be put together, but if you ever again spout your opinions about the mixing of the races to this here man, who I love deeply, you and I are going to have us a little problem."

As I make my way back to my place at the other end of the table, Uncle Earl booms into the deathly silence, "So Julio, tell me about them gators y'all say you got in that big ole lake where that thar canal is lo-cated."

Buckets of adrenalin still coursing through me, I'm not that hungry when the heaps of food arrive. I watch Julio taste the fried okra and the greens. As my family murmurs encouragement, I show him how to add hot vinegar and crumble his cornbread into the turnips to sop up the pot liquor. But all the while I'm keeping an eye on Uncle Walter as he wolfs down his meat loaf and leaves the table while the rest of us are still filling in the corners of our hunger. The adrenalin having seeped from my tired body, my anger has been overshadowed by a feeling of intense sadness. Just as I feared in bringing Julio here, I have chosen to do something which has disappointed someone I love. It doesn't matter right now who is right and who is wrong. I'm just sad. I'm not naive enough to think the war is over either. This was just the opening skirmish, a shot fired across the bow. Uncle may have retreated temporarily, but this ain't over. Not by a country mile.

GOO GOO BARS

This recipe came from Aunt Pauline. As you might expect the candy was my favorite as a child. I can't remember a single birthday when someone didn't give me a box of Goo Goo bars. The Piggly Wiggly stopped carrying them when I was still in grade school, but Miss Wynonna kept them behind the candy counter of The Southern Pride for years. Just for me, she said, though I realize now she probably sold them to other folks. What child could resist such a sweet mess with her own name printed boldly on the white and red wrapper?

Ingredients

2 T butter
1 can Eagle Brand sweetened condensed milk
12 oz bag of milk chocolate chips
2 c roasted peanuts (Auntie sometimes substitutes pecans)
2 c miniature marshmallows

Melt butter, milk and chocolate in double boiler or microwave. Stir in nuts and marshmallows just enough to blur but not completely blend the marshmallows. Press into a buttered 9x13 inch pan and refrigerate about an hour.

Aunt Pauline always let me sit at the kitchen table and lick clean her long handled wooden spoon and heavy yellow mixing bowl. Descended into a sugary bliss I would invariably forget her instructions and swing my feet to and fro, kicking the leg of her Grandma Burnett's table. Auntie swears that table is permanently marked with the proof of my incorrigible cuteness.

Chapter Four ★

The sisters, Baby Ruth and Snickers, get together and decide that Julio and I should ride from The Cracker Barrel just outside Atlanta all the way to Noisy Creek in the back seat of a silver Bentley.

"I commandeered this here chunk of ostentatious metal special for you Goo Goo," Aunt Snickers confides to me as we head across the parking lot hand in hand. "I told Preston this morning that nothing was gonna do but that he let me drive you home in this vee-hicle."

I squeeze Auntie's hand and she leans in and confides, "I figured to let your Julio know that we Noisy Creek folks enjoy the luxurious things in life right along with his own kin."

"Who is this man you are engaged to?" I ask when I see the sleek Bentley wedged in between Uncle Hershel's twelve year old jeep Wrangler and Uncle Clark's classic Pontiac Firebird.

"Oh Lord Goo Goo," Aunt Snickers shakes her head, "I just love the stuffin' out a the man, but he has got more money than good sense about half the time."

The Bentley smells like leather soap and Auntie Snicker's Joy perfume. I decide not to ask why her signature scent hangs so heavily in the backseat. My confrontation with Uncle Walter has left me hollowed out and exhausted. Auntie hasn't even maneuvered the car out of the parking lot before I've snuggled into Julio's shoulder and dropped into sleep.

The last thing I hear is Aunt Snickers asking Julio if this is his first trip to the United States of America. By the time Julio is half way through his tactful answer that his family comes to the states a few times a year but he has never before had the opportunity to visit this lovely part of the country, I am sinking into a memory of a sweaty young girl following her uncle through the piney woods of home.

In the dream, I smell the smoke of a campfire overlaid with bacon. I am snuggled into my warm sleeping bag and refuse to pull myself out into the frosty air. When I finally crawl out of my blue mummy bag, the sun has burned all the white from the grass and Uncle Walter is frying eggs in the old cast iron frying pan. Over a leisurely breakfast, Uncle lectures me on the rules of deer hunting—never take anything but a clean head or heart shot and never leave the hunt until a wounded animal had been located and killed. The taste of farm raised bacon still sweet in my mouth, I pack the frying pan down to the creek and scour it clean with fine gravel. When I get back to camp, Uncle hands me my rifle and we head out of camp.

There isn't a breath of breeze once we step into the trees. Uncle follows a deer trail that winds its way through the thick pines. I follow Uncle. The needles are thick under our leather boots, muffling our steps as we climb slowly toward the ridge. My grand-daddy's old Winchester bolt action .30-06 is heavy in my arms, sweat rolls down my back and with each chigger bite I question God's love. Just behind Uncle Walter and slightly to his left, out of the corner of my eye, I catch movement. I stop dead still, turn my head slowly like I've been taught, study the place where I felt the air stir.

The buck is looking directly at me. A dead oak stag is behind him so that there's no way to visually separate antler from bare branches. But, his stance and musculature give him away as a prime male. I do not have a scope on my rifle. In fact, while I have deer tags, they are always used by one of the uncles. But, even without a clear view of his antlers, I know this is a buck. As we stand across from each other and stare into each other's eyes I have the eerie feeling that he has come, right to this spot, just for me. Uncle Walter has worked his way back to me. He follows my line of sight to the deer, the animal still frozen no more than fifty feet from where we both stand transfixed.

To shoot I have to slide the bolt of the .30-06 open and then bring it forward to push a bullet into the chamber. I know Uncle carries his rifle locked and loaded, the safety switch its only prevention against accidental shooting. I understand that, while I have spotted this buck, my uncle will take the shot. He might give me a nod by putting my tag on the deer, but the shot is his. While these details streak through my head, Uncle Walter and I and the buck stand locked together in that dark wood, all of us quivering with anticipation. Some moments in life expand, become deeper, longer than the second hand on a watch will report.

Uncle's deep voice is a whisper in the still air telling me to take the shot. I grew up helping to butcher hogs and calves, rabbits and chickens. I remember to press the .30.06 hard against my shoulder. The noise when I slide the bolt is like a crack of thunder in the deep quiet of the piney green, and still, that buck stands and stares into his fate as I sight along the Winchester's barrel.

Concentrating so fully on the gentle squeeze of the trigger, the sound of the shot nearly stops my heart as well as the buck's. Then Uncle Walter is whooping and crashing through the brush that separates us from the fallen deer and I am stumbling after his broad back, the Winchester so tight in my hand I know my fingers will be sore the next day from the pressure. My shot has entered the deer's head almost exactly centered between his eyes. I stand over the carcass, stare down at those eyes that mere seconds before seemed joined with mine in a union of life. The deep peace of the woods recedes leaving just me and the result of a slight increase in pressure on the trigger of Grand-daddy's old Winchester.

I begin to shake, a five second warning that I am going to vomit up my breakfast eggs. Uncle Walter hands me an old handkerchief, instructs me to wipe my mouth, I still have work to do. He passes me his antler handled deer knife and I slit the buck's throat to allow the blood to drain. Uncle grins at me.

"He's too big to carry. I'll go back to camp and fetch us some rope. We'll dress him out here," he's already turning away when he hesitates and calls back over his shoulder, "You ok to stay here while I go back?"

I slide the bolt on the .30-06, set the safety, just in case an old black bear or some such comes looking for an easy meal, call back loud and clear just as though I'm not still shaking inside like a little girl, "You go ahead. I'm ok here.

I think that, in the dream, I stay right there in that moment, alone with that dead buck, the air already thick with the buzz of black flies, all the way from Atlanta to just outside Hunley Mountain when Julio wakes me by speaking my name softly and rubbing his warm hand across my cheek, bringing me back into what most would call the real world.

I rub my eyes, stretch my arms over my head and arch my back to stretch out the kinks. Aunt Snickers has the sun roof open on the Bentley and the heady blend of kudzu, red dirt and pine trees make me feel like I am breathing naturally for the first time in years. Standing up in the backseat so that my head and shoulders stick out through the sunroof   I let loose a rebel yell or two.

"Get your rowdy self back inside this car right now!" Aunt Snickers scolds, "afore your Auntie Ruth is forced to cut the tangles right on out a that wild hair of yours."

Plopping down in the seat beside Julio, I give him a belated welcome to Georgia kiss and try to see this scrubby land the way Julio is seeing it. For me, every snaking creek, every dirt road winding up into the hills, every barbeque joint and Dairy Queen is memory gilded.

Down that dirt road we're just now passing is the foot path to the creek where we all went skinny dipping after the Senior Prom. Julio is perceiving scrub pine and red dirt. I'm seeing moonlight on white flesh, titillating flashes of rounded buttocks and smooth backs. I'm reliving sheltering in a small cave. Samuel's eighteen year old body taunt under mine as we listened to the music of the creek just a few feet below us. Samuel and I had been closing in on sex for two years, like two kids inexpertly chasing a prize butterfly through familiar woods, we'd nearly have it in our net and then we'd lose our nerve at the moment of capture. That night, my lavender prom dress hanging from the branches of a pine tree swaying in the night breeze like a voyeur, we managed to capture the prize.

In the back seat of the Bentley, breathing deeply of the smells of home, these memories seem to me a part of the air, invisible mist that hangs in every crevasse, the land itself damp with the seepage of personal history, shrouded in the fog of the past. Try as I might, I cannot see Noisy Creek without a wash of love and memories coloring my perceptions.

"What do you think of Georgia so far?" I ask Julio.

He kisses the inside of my wrist, declares firmly, "I believe here you are more light and also more full than you are in Panama."

For someone who has a little trouble with the language, the man has a way with words. He's right. I am lighter here. In Noisy Creek I am familiar with every nuance, every molecule of air having been recycled by my blood kin. There are few surprises in the landscape and even the changes I do notice—a few new houses, land cleared here, a new barn there—these have a solid base in the past. This is home. I have no need to use any part of my brain whatsoever to decipher the behavior or culture of the people around me. This sense of belonging, fitting with my surrounding, does indeed make me both lighter and fuller.

Julio and I are staying at the house on Clanton Lane, my Aunt Ruth's home for all the years that I've been alive. She and Johnny Goodin lived here until he died a few years back, another of Auntie's husbands dead in the middle of lighting a few personal fireworks. Her first husband died in the Vietnam War. Her second, Billy Martin, actually died of melanoma skin cancer, but the legend is that Auntie eased him into paradise by providing a good bit of wifely comfort at the moment of death. Johnny B. Goodin also died while making love to Auntie, probably in the very bed that Julio and I will be sharing tonight. A fact I have neglected to mention to Julio. Noisy Creek has enough living, fire breathing folks he has to contend with. No need for him to deal with the multitude of ghosts among us with whom we locals are accustomed to living.

The Aunties have stocked the refrigerator with iced tea, fried chicken, peach pie and what looks like both collards and turnip greens. The message light on the answering machine is flashing with twenty eight missed calls. When it was discovered that my cell phone will require a trip to radio shack before it will work in the U. S. of A, several folks offered me the loan of theirs, but I am purposely staying out of touch for a day or two. I have spent the last eighteen months in my own self-made world. Even when Julio and I dragged ourselves out of bed and socialized, most of his friends speak English as a second language. It was an extra step for them to include me in the conversation. I became adept at being on the edge of social activity, grew to enjoy a certain lazy sporadic involvement that left me free to think my own thoughts, to be an observer rather than a participant. Here in Noisy Creek, I am smack dab in the middle of things. Being an active participant in the drama of daily life is mandated by Barr Family Law.

Julio, working as he does in his family's business, is accustomed to being constantly surrounded by people demanding a piece of his attention. He, bless his heart, seems to be adjusting more easily than I to our arrival in my home town. I pour him a glass of tea and we sit on the sun room glider and watch the pearly light of dusk filter through the glossy leaves of the magnolias. I've called Aunt Ruth and asked her to spread the word that I'm exhausted and just want a good night's sleep breathing the air of my childhood. We'll start catching up tomorrow.

My feet tucked under me, my head on Julio's broad shoulder, I am aware of a dullness in the quality of light here as compared to the shimmer of tropical air to which I've grown accustomed. As quickly as that awareness strikes, I am crying, grieving for my past when I had no basis for comparison and was thus firm in my belief in Noisy Creek as the most beautiful place in the world. That this grief may be misplaced pain over my estrangement from my beloved and obstinate Uncle Walter does occur to me, but I choose to smash that thought down with the remnants of my anger.

"You are sad?" Julio kisses my forehead, strokes my hair with a look of puzzled concern on his handsome face.

"When I was in Panama," I whimper pathetically, "I was, really every second of every day, homesick for this place. Now I am home and I am yearning for Panama."

His smile is warm and soft, makes me want to fold myself into him and stay forever.

"This is not a problem," he tells me, "It means only that you are a woman."

I pull back from him, flash a warning which only causes his smile to widen.

"Do not now become like fire. I tell you the truth. You want everything, yes?"

I can only nod.

"Maybe you and I, we will make this happen. We will find a way for you to have everything. My country and yours also."

I know what he's offering. He and I joined together. We could live part time in each country, fly back and forth at will. But wanting something doesn't make it possible. Uncle Walter's little speech at The Cracker Barrel has made me confront a hard truth of my own. Is it possible that the reason I chose Julio to begin with and then kept him at arm's length for as long as I did was at least partially because of a prejudice of my own? Did I see him as a dark-skinned plaything, a boy toy if you will, despite his intellect and goodness and success in his own country? Was my perception of him heavily flavored by an ingrained cultural bias of my own? It's not just Uncle Walter who's a product of his background and system of beliefs which has stood him in reasonably good stead for his whole life. Lots of things hold pretty darn firm until you start poking at 'em with a big stick.

I'm sure my thinking of big sticks has nothing to do with Julio's kissing my neck, nuzzling softly on my earlobe. Nevertheless, I push him away for a moment. I want his undivided attention and all the blood circulating in our big brains.

"How did you do this morning with Uncle Walter's little spiel at the restaurant?"

"He is your tio. He loves you. This is not a problem. I will speak with him."

I don't like the idea of Julio talking with Uncle Walter, can imagine a dozen ways such a conversation might make the situation worse than it already is. But, while Julio's words are spoken softly, his tone makes it clear that he is not asking my permission for such a conversation.

I tell him that Uncle Walter taught me to hunt. That I have spent many hours in the woods walking or sitting quietly beside him while we swatted black flies and gnats and waited for a careless buck to walk into our sites. I try to explain that other hunters, even many of my uncles, put out salt licks, even use doe scent, to trick a buck into coming out into the open. They sit in tower blinds, sip whisky spiked coffee and watch the bait until they can line up a shot. Uncle Walter considers this way of hunting dishonorable.

I explain that with Uncle Walter I learned to recognize a particular deer by the way he placed his feet, to study a 'V' track in the mud or on the incline of a creek bed and to know weight and age and health of the animal who made it. It was Uncle who taught me to stand silently in the woods and hear its secrets. The marks on a tree where a buck had rubbed his velvet antlers. The oval pattern of barely flattened ferns that told of a doe bedding with her fawns. I learned to poke around in the round pellets of deer droppings to find what the buck was feeding on in order to know where he would be in the early morning and late afternoons.

With my head on Julio's shoulder and tears wetting my face, I tell how Uncle and I usually found the buck we were tracking. We almost always lined up a clear shot. But we rarely took the shot. Most years we brought back empty tags. We tracked for that one moment that seemed to stretch into eternity, when we sighted down the barrel of a rifle and shared the power of the animal. That instantaneous glimpse into eternity when the deer's life was vulnerable to the slightest pressure of our finger on a small curved slice of metal and we were joined with the buck.

Telling all this to Julio I blush at the self revelation, wonder if Julio is going to think I'm nuttier than Aunt Enid's Christmas fruit cake.

He nods his head matter-of-factly. "Yes. Mano a mano," he tells me. "Like the bull and the matador, yes?"

I've never thought of that comparison, but agree that he may be correct. His next insight though, surprises me.

"A person who can look into the eyes of his opponent and kill honorably, with a knife is I think more better, but with a gun also is true, that person is rare, yes? That person is worthy of respect."

We sit quietly in the dark until I am struck by another difference between Noisy Creek and Panama City.

"No car alarms!" I exclaim.

"No horns," Julio adds, "I do not know how you drive here."

With that I make a crude comment about honking his horn and we begin the dance that will lead us down the hall and onto the bed where Johnny Goodin first saw God face to face.

Afterward we stand naked in the light of the open door of the refrigerator. Neither of us have unpacked yet. Julio because he has never in his life packed or unpacked a suitcase for himself. Me because I'm just too darn lazy to do the work tonight. I pull out thick plates of fried chicken and deep bowls of greens pop them in the microwave just as they come from the refrigerator shelf. We sit at the wooden table where I once sat with a magnifying glass and a clip-on table lamp and built a model of a butterfly attaching thorax to abdomen, labial palp to the top of the head, while Aunt Ruth stirred up a batch of butter cream cookies with chocolate sprinkles.

Tonight the only light is ambient from the lamp post hidden in the leaves of the magnolia. Julio has found a pan of cornbread behind the peach pie and we crumble it into our warm turnip greens. By the time we're finished, I have chicken grease over roughly fifty percent of my body. Julio appears to have not one drop of grease on even his soft mouth. I need a shower but Julio suggests we get dressed and go out on the town.

"Honey what town? There isn't anything open in Noisy Creek at this hour."

"Yes," he insists, "it is not yet ten o'clock. We go for a drink and maybe a little dancing, yes?"

"No," I laugh, "we do not. Reb's Café and Goggins Barbeque both close at 9:00 and there are no bars in Noisy Creek. It's a dry county."

Which is how we nearly end my first night home as gator food.

I dig through my backpack for jeans and an old gray t-shirt. Julio locates, on the bottom of the smallest piece of luggage, just as the list provided by his sainted mother promises, what he calls his play clothes—chinos, a long sleeved cotton shirt and a pair of ostrich skin cowboy boots. I drive the old truck Uncle Neil left for us in Aunt Ruth's garage. Flashes of the road are visible through the holes in the floorboards and the transmission has lost third, but it gets us out to just past Sinclair's orchard all right.

I park under the spreading branches of a Sweet Gum and we pick our way by the bluish light of a crescent moon through the dark trunks of the peach and apple trees. Within minutes we are being followed by the Sinclair's watch dog, a little brown and white terrier mix. I find the trail I'm looking for, the one that leads to the trespasser's swimming hole that Mr. Sinclair built years back by diverting a year round trickle of muddy creek water into a rock dammed irrigation pond. The red mud path has eroded some since the last time I was here. We slide down the steep embankment on our butts, my laughter and Julio's surprised gasps mixing with the excited yips of the terrier and bouncing off the steep ochre cliffs on the opposite side of the swimming hole.

The moon is hidden behind a gray horse tail of cloud. We've already shed our clothes and are wading out into the thick water before my eyes have completely adjusted to the darkness. The mossy length of a tree, flood swept from an eroded bank further up stream catches my eye as the water inches up our bare bellies. My feet are sunk in muck up to my ankles, my legs and ass quickly succumb to the numbing power of muddy water just slightly warmer than the air into which our gasps make little clouds—short, rapid bursts of exhale like choo choo trains on an ill advised mountain track. My exposed breasts and shoulders are chicken skinned. With one hand on Julio's shivering chest, I prepare to sink into the water up to my neck in an attempt to avoid the cold breeze coming off the surface of the water.

My grin is making my cold cheeks ache. I am, as my Great Aunt Selma has told me countless times, as happy as if I had good sense. This is the moment when I see that hoary log undulating toward us. It takes this ole Georgia girl less than a millisecond to process this phenomenon. What I mistakenly thought was a waterlogged length of wood is, in fact, a hungry alligator moving leisurely toward Julio's gorgeous bare ass. Now I know that gators don't generally attack people, but they do have a powerful taste for small dogs. Especially small yappy dogs and the Sinclair's terrier hasn't shut up since he joined us.

The gator will go straight for the dog. The problem is, Julio and I are butt naked in direct line between the gator and the non-stop yips of the terrier. I'm pretty sure that, if we just stay out of the way, we won't be in any danger. But I feel responsible for the dog and while my Uncle Walter taught me to hunt, it was my Uncle Earl who was my childhood guide on the local lakes and rivers. This ain't my first nighttime encounter with a hungry gator.

A sliver of moon is now exposed between the wispy clouds. Just enough cold light to reflect from the yellow reptilian eyes now less than thirty feet from Julio's exposed backside. I can't see any large branches or rocks within reach that I might use as a weapon. Then, in an epiphany, I remember Julio's ostrich skin boots. The gator is still coming on. It's hard to tell how big an alligator is when he's submerged in tannic brown water on a nearly moonless night. Also, I assure myself, the fear factor alone is probably doubling his girth and length. A vibration like a tuning fork resonates at that low place in my gut where primitive fear resides. My head knows the gator is coming right at us only because the dog is directly behind us. My gut is screaming at me to get our asses out of the water. Now!

My other little problem is how to tell my city boy lover that an alligator is headed our way without causing him to thrash around like a wounded catfish turning the gator's attention from the morsel of dogmeat he is hunting to the larger sweetmeat feast in front of him. This particular problem is complicated by the fact that, cold or no cold, Julio is having his usual reaction to seeing my boobs. Keeping my eye on the gator, I reach for Julio's hand and find another appendage entirely. This isn't helping our situation. Finally, I opt for the direct approach and simply order Julio, in my best drill sergeant voice, to walk calmly and quickly out of the water and go to the left, as far away from the yipping dog as he can get. Six sisters and a bossy, if sainted, mother—the man follows my directions instinctively.

I walk backward to where our clothes are piled, never taking my eyes from that lumpy head, bend sideways until I have a death grip on a boot top. By this time Julio has realized I am not behind him. He turns and starts back toward me just as the gator's head lunges out of the dark water toward the still barking dog. I slam the boot sidewise, the pointy toe catching the gator behind one iridescent gold eye. The beast isn't deterred, nor does he seem amused. He turns that flat head toward me. I have a fraction of a second, a lifetime, to think that hitting an alligator in the head with an ostrich skin cowboy boot will be my last stupid act on this earth. Then a .30-30 explodes into the night, shatters the moment, kills the gator and causes me to wet my naked self.

Before the urine has warmed my knees, Julio is between me and the now dead gator, trying to shield me from the lake monster as well as from the glint of the rifle barrel above us.

"Evening Mr. Sinclair," I call up the embankment.

"Baby Ruth Barr," Hugh Sinclair calls to us. "Is that you standing down yonder naked as a jay bird in my gator pond?"

"It's Goo Goo Barr, Mr. Sinclair, Baby Ruth's niece. I've got my beau here with me. I was showing him what we do for excitement here abouts."

The flashlight beam moves from Julio's exposed body, to the eight or nine foot length of dead gator, then back up to my face peering over the top of Julio's shoulder.

"Y'all bring your young buck on up to house now. Miss Nancy'll get'cha some hot cocoa and peach pie."

"Yes sir," I call up as the flashlight beam swings away from us.

Mr. Sinclair's laughter drowns out even the infernal yipping of the little watch dog. The man stops a few yards into the trees, turns the beam of light back toward us, illuminating me as I'm struggling to get my wet legs into my jeans, lets the flashlight play a bit over my bare skin.

"Good to see ya again Goo Goo," he chuckles before leaving us alone in the dark with the dead gator.

Chapter Five

It's only the end of September but the first frost has already ended the life cycle of the fireflies for another year. Travellers Park is chuck full of my relatives when I park Uncle Earl's beater under a spreading oak along rural route four and Julio and I pick our way through the goatheads along the side of the road. I'm packing a serving dish of chicken and rice which I've cooked with adobo and Panamanian cilantro. Julio's contribution we bought from the back of an eighteen wheeler hidden up in the piney woods just across the county line. He has a case of Jax up on one shoulder and he's been seen by the uncles several of whom are headed our way.

I am wearing my favorite pair of jeans and a purple t-shirt with 'Pipa' in green letters across my breasts. Julio has on new chinos, a burgundy striped cotton shirt and his gator killers. Uncle Neil is in the lead coming toward us across the meadow. Not surprising since the man has been known to drive across three states, fill a horse trailer with Jax and then race back from Beaumont, Texas like a modern day moonshiner.

Uncle is wearing the same orange tank top with the stretched arm holes he wore when pontificating with Matt Lauder on the precise degree of rottenness of the gator meat he used to hook into a record breaking Gar. I missed this bit of hometown drama being out of the country, but Aunt Snickers sent me a link to the Today Show footage.

My favorite part of the interview was the look on Lauder's face as Uncle lectured that, "Y'all want a fine coating a dark green along the surface a the meat and when you open the cooler the o-door should be enough to bring some water into yer eyes but not so much so as to actually cause you to upchuck."

Uncle Earl, of course, is in Dickie overalls and his battered and stained Braves cap.

His growl rumbles across the grass while we're still a hundred yards out, "Ah am deeply wounded that y'all didn't call me to go moonlight gator wrestling with you."

When we get close enough, he takes a gander at my t-shirt and asks, "Pipa? That ain't some Yankee thang is it?"

I kiss his scratchy cheek.

"It's coconut water, Uncle. A favorite in Panama."

I hug Uncle Neil's neck and hand off the pan of chicken and rice to Uncle Earl. I've been told there is now Wi-fi internet right here in Travellers Park and I've brought my laptop so I can show my slides to all the relatives at once of 'that godforsaken place y'all left us to go and explore.'

Uncle Neil comes with me when I tell him I'm fetching my computer. He explains that when Aunt Ruth's new husband, Collin, put up a tower so the folks out at his Green Acres development could get internet access, he put up a relay tower as well so that most of Noisy Creek now has wireless internet free of charge. While I'm still blinking from Uncle's knowledge of wireless connections and relay stations, he tells me that he and Uncle Earl have gone in together and bought themselves a computer.

"If our favor-ite niece is gonna live the other end a the world, her old uncles has got to be able to keep in touch."

I don't ask about the internet porn they also have available through the miracle of technology, but cynic that I am, I have a slight suspicion that access to sites with names like Girls Gone Down and Big Boobies may have played a role in the decision as well.

"I saw you on TV with your record breaking Gar." I change the subject.

"They had that on the TV way down yonder in the jungle?"

I actually watched it on the computer while sitting on Julio's leather sofa sipping a diet coke and munching whole wheat crackers and Brie, but I just nod my head. Sometimes the pictures folks have in their heads are better than reality.

"Yep." Uncle does his best to look modest, "That thar fish was a biggun."

I wait for him to elaborate thinking maybe this is why he's insisted on walking me back to the truck to get my computer.

But he only adds, "Don't mention it to yer Uncle Earl. That done pissed him off to no end. Me catchin' that Gar Fish."

There is no mistaking the malicious joy in his voice and I poke him in the ribs with my elbow.

"We're getting a new statue," he confides getting to the real reason for the escort.

The story, as it unravels, is that Preston Yates, Aunt Snickers' new man friend, is donating a bronze. Since we already have what some might say is an overabundance of statuary in Noisy Creek, I'm confused by this generous donation.

Downtown Confederate Square has the standard Rebel Boy in Tattered Gray that keeps his lonely vigil in nearly every town south of the Mason Dixon. Lee Park has a bronze of the great and honorable General Lee. We've got Jeff Davis standing eternal guard out on what is now Martin Luther King Boulevard and right here at Travellers Park stands the equestrian statue of General Lee and his near sacred horse, Traveller.

When I mention this to Uncle, he asks, "Member how y'all got yourself in trouble in Miss Morehouse's Sunday school class by sayin' as how the first thang y'all wanted to do once ya stepped inside the pearly gates was to hug the neck a ole Traveller and slip him a sugar cube or two?"

"I remember you told her the idea gave you a mind to keep a few sugar cubes in your pocket just in case the good lord called you unexpected like. So, what's this new statue going to be?"

"Miss Bessie Smith," Uncle declares triumphantly and I understand that this is the heart of the gossip.

"Bessie Smith? The fictional old lady hero in the mythical Battle of Noisy Creek?"

"That there's the story all right."

"Where's this new bronze going to go?" I ask as I slip the shoulder strap of my laptop case over Uncle's shoulder and we head back to the park.

"In our brand new hundred acre city park at the base a Martin's Ridge. Except it's gonna be called Yatesville, if'n Mr. Yates has his way. The most interesting thang though is that the statue is gonna be created by none other than that little ole prissy daughter a his. Kristen Yates."

"This is the girl that was chasin' after Collin when he and Aunt Ruth were first getting together?"

"Ah yep. That little gal didn't know what hit her once your Aunt Ruth stood up on her hind quarters and let her rip."

I've heard this story from a dozen or so folks via international phone call, letter and e-mail. Evidently Aunt Ruth drove the girl to Atlanta and put her on a plane back to California. Word is the California gal was lucky to get away with her life.

I cut my eyes over to Uncle, raise one eyebrow to encourage him to elaborate, but he only grunts and tells me, "Yep. That thar little gal is a piece a work."

The proposed Bessie Smith Recreational Area is the talk of the party. Aunt Snickers and Preston Yates are not in attendance. Gossip has them in Monaco with a European princess, but Aunt Ruth tells me they're in L.A. fighting over the statue's design with his daughter Kristen.

"The girl has been attending some art college in California. Preston says she's gotten real good," Aunt Ruth says in a voice that alerts me that she has some doubt herself as to just whether this child can be trusted to create a statue that the whole bunch of us is going to be stuck with for the rest of our natural lives.

"I'm sure Aunt Snickers will keep a close eye on things," I assure Aunt Ruth.

"One would hope. But Kristen is mighty secretive when it suits her," Aunt Ruth kisses my check, looks around Travellers Park and adds, "For sure the announcement of the park and the statue is gonna give folks something to discuss."

I could hug Aunt Snickers neck for choosing this moment to spring the news on everyone. The focus of the torches and pitchforks hasn't been turned this successfully from one family member to another since Janet Jackson exposed her nipple on national television and drew the media frenzy away from her pervert brother.

The family is divided between those who think the park and statue are a generous offer which will enrich our community and for which we should be grateful, and those who know a bribe when they smell one. This second opinion being the one held by everyone except Aunt Ruth. Nevertheless, I would bet good money that, within a year, Aunt Ruth's judgment will be the predominantly held public view. Privately folks will still whisper about Carpetbaggers and folks so crooked they have to screw their socks on, and there will still exist a little underground guerrilla war that nobody but a local will even know to recognize. But publicly folks will get on board. Because the park will indeed be a nice addition to the community and because there's not a damn thing we can do about it.

Preston Yates, or as he's more commonly known, that rich son of bitch, bought up a chunk of Noisy Creek history that we took for granted for over a hundred years. I suppose the city could have purchased Martin's Ridge for a little bit of nothing years ago. Even now, Mr. Yates didn't pay the Martin's much for the rugged mountain land we always said was too steep to be good for much except goats, White Tail and the local cash crop.

"I never thought of that mountain as having any more potential then as a place where you could shoot a buck on the ridge and have it roll all the way to the creek bed if you weren't mighty careful," Uncle Walter allows.

An hour later Julio and Uncle Walter are skipping stones across the rain swelled creek. If they don't seem particularly friendly, at least they aren't chucking the rocks at each other. I wander down to join them, link my arms through theirs and walk the both of them back to where Uncle Earl is holding court and frying up what everyone has taken to calling 'Goo Goo's attack gator.'

Hugh and Nancy Sinclair are here. Nancy, who makes the hands down best peach cobbler in town, has brought us a sample of her prizewinning delicacy and Hugh is embellishing the story of how his beauty sleep was disturbed by the racket of that damn dawg yipping and carrying on.

"I fetched up my .30-30 from the bedside and grabbed up my flashlight from off'n the nightstand where I always keep it in case of a power outage. Once I was outside I just followed the noise of the infernal yipping and yapping. I'll be a ring-tailed cat if'n I didn't discover myself a couple a naked trespassers needing rescuing from that ole yeller gator that's been sneaking in to rob my trot lines in the night."

Julio appears to be taking all this in stride. Of course it's entirely possible that what with the accent and all, he doesn't actually understand much of what's being said. I don't know whether to hug on him to demonstrate to my family that I am deeply fond of this man, an action which I know for a fact is going to arouse bad feelings in a good many of my relatives, or to keep myself chaste and sisterly around him in order to not rile up the bigotry. Finally I give up and decide to just act normal, though admittedly, when one has to think about how to act normal, things come off less than plumb line straight.

The subject keeps swinging back to the new park and statue. Some folks are of the opinion that Preston Yates isn't so much generous as smart.

My Uncle Nougat hikes his jeans, runs a thumbnail along his week old beard and opines, "That man ain't no dummy. Putting in that big ole park right there as you turn up the ridge to those fancy mansions he's building for them rich folks who, by the by, we can all expect to have invading our homes and restaurants with their high fallutin' ways."

I can't think of a single reason why rich folk would come into our homes and Noisy Creek has a barbeque shack and two café's, all three of which serve the best food on God's green earth, but which seem to me unlikely to attract folks looking for fine linen and gourmet cuisine.

"What about all those houses out in Leeville. Green Acres. How have those folks affected the town?" I ask.

These are the ecologically green houses built by Aunt Ruth's new husband. I know for a fact that the new home owners have added to the coffers of the town's tax roles

and churches and caused a second Reb's Café to go in out
at that end of town. The consensus of opinion that's made
its way to Panama is that these new folks are a downright
blessing to the town. My hope in asking the question is to
remind folks that new people moving into the area are not
necessarily a threat to our redneck way of life.

Aunt Ruth winks at me over the top of the hunk of
gator she's daintily nibbling. Sitting on a folding lawn
chair right beside me she squeezes my hand. The two of
us are fooling no one with our collusion. Collin, the
creator of Green Acres, can be seen stealing second base
from Bobby Foster in the pickup game going on out under
the thick branches of the magnolias.

Aunt Minnie puts an end to the comparison when
she declares, "Them Green Acres newcomers is plain
honest folks. Country people mostly who been forced to
live in the city to support their families. They'se retired
outta the city now and glad to be here. You wait and see,
these here new people have got mo' money than they got
brains. This here is gonna be a bad match."

True to Barr tradition there are six long folding
tables set up under the overhanging branches of the
Maples and Magnolias. Great grandma Barr's picnic linen
is mostly hidden by covered dishes. The mix of these
tables has changed some since I was kid. Used to be we'd
have three tables of heavy main dishes—buttermilk fried
chicken and pork loin, pineapple studded hams and
smoked turkeys, two and a half tables of desserts, with
two token salads set up at the end of the second dessert
table. The placement was essential to allow us all to

waddle past the bowl of lettuce and the snap top Tupperware of sliced fruit only after we'd come back for our second or third helping of dessert.

I'd have me a mighty tall heap of change if I had a nickel for every time one of my aunts staggered past a bowl of wilting greens and declared, "Why here is the salad I was huntin'. Well dang, it is just too late now to worry about my diet."

Today's gathering has a full table of salads and we have a seventh table set up beside the parks only electrical outlet. There's an electrical strip with receptacles for fourteen plugs with tangled black cords like a passel of breeding snakes weaving from the plug to the table on which are spread eight lap tops. Two of these belong to my cousins Billy Bob Foster and Cooter Clark who, in my absence have become day traders.

An interesting career move since, when I left eighteen months ago, it was a badly kept secret that these two had the county's biggest crop of Georgia Gold up on Martin's Ridge. Seeing the two of them there, hunched over their computers, their faces intent, as though the world turned on the next stroke of their previously guano smelling fingers, it hits me why some folks are upset about Preston Yates' mountain development.

As I set up my Sony, Cooter folds his Mac closed as if protecting state secrets and tells me, "We high tech rednecks now, Cousin."

I start the show on its endless loop. My plan is to leave the slides running for whoever strolls past to watch for as long as they want. The first picture on the screen shows cutter ants marching in a seemingly endless line across the jungle floor. Each tiny insect has one delicate cream colored flower held tightly in its mandibles where the blossom sways above its head. The ants look to me like a parade of tiny bridesmaids stretching into a green infinity. Aunt Maude wants to hear all about how the harvest ants carry the flowers back to the ant hill where farmer ants use it to make the fungus on which the entire colony then feeds. Aunt Enid asks where the little flowers come from. I explain that they are from the Teak Tree whose mass of blooms look like basket ball sized bunches of Baby's Breath.

The photos flash on the screen and I listen to my aunties exclaim, "Lord have mercy, I just nevah imagined such a thang as that" and field questions like, "So they got themselves electricity down thar then, huh?" and "I declare did y'all ever see so many a them tall buildings? Aren't ya a-feared they'll collapse around your ears while your sleepin'?" The last picture is one I took from Ancon Hill with the city framed by dense jungle and spread out in a crescent along the blue water. By the time I get to it the Georgia sky is a wash of apricot over pearly gray and dusk is settling over the park.

Julio has long ago joined the baseball game. His gator killers being unsuitable for running bases, he's been outfitted with a pair of my Cousin Eddie's tennis shoes. I've been watching him from the corner of my eye while providing a running commentary on the slide show. He seems to have started the game as a short stop but has now taken over the position of first base. There are a near equal number of girl cousins out on the field with the guys working up a sweat. I never have been good at, or much interested in sports, making me an oddity among the young cousins.

Tracking animals or bird and butterfly watching in the woods, swimming in the creek, or just hiking in the mountains are my loves. Uncle Walter used to tell folks that I found anything that involved chasing or throwing or running with a ball to be as useless as tits on a boar hawg while anything that got me out into the woods was better than a tent revival. He was right. Julio though seems to be proving himself to be a fine ballplayer. He's up to bat now and I can hear my cousin Sharlene heckling him from her spot at third base, "This Battah cain't hit. He ain't no Rod Carew!"

I grin and wave to Sharlene. I understand that razzing Julio is her way of showing support, offsetting the quiet stares and awkward silences coming from some of my other cousins. I'm real clear as to the significance of the Stars and Bars that Cousin Mason has deemed it necessary to retrieve from his mud splattered truck and stretch across the makeshift backstop of blue plastic.

Sharlene's mama, my Aunt Enid, walks past with a plate heaped with fried chicken and potato salad. She pats me on the shoulder and tells me kindly, "Them folks is good athletes, ain't nobody can say no different."

I decide to take the comment in the spirit in which it is intended.

Listening to the bits and pieces of conversation around me, I can't help but grin. I had forgotten how we all, the whole bunch of us Barrs and Clarks and Fosters and Ragsdales and Martins and Goodins, when we get together, we fall back on our linguistic roots. There's not a one of us that can't speak like the educated folks we are. But when we congregate we're like those sets of quadruplets that have their own secret language. I'm pretty sure it serves the same purpose too—excludes the outsiders while bonding us together.

My Aunt Enid has gingerly settled her bulk in the chair next to me. The chair is one of those folding contraptions with nylon strips stretched across aluminum rods. Stretched being the key word at the moment. She reaches her hand up to take mine as I stand watching the baseball game.

"What does your Julio do for a living, Dear?" she asks. The heads of four aunts and six uncles sitting along the table bench to the left of us, turn just slightly at this question. Conversation falters, confirms Auntie's recon mission.

"He works in his family's business. They have an interest in a couple of banks, a few department stores and restaurants. That kind of thing."

I can almost see the wheels turning in the heads of my relatives. I wait for it. Stare out at the ballgame where Julio is on second base, count to one hundred and six before Uncle Jackie politely dribbles tobacco juice into his portable spittoon, a Spam can with one rounded corner custom contoured to his grizzled chin, and grunts, "He ain't some kind a Drug Lord is he?"

I think of trying to explain that Julio's family traces its ancestry back to King Ferdinand, that they are respected business people, politically and economically powerful. I think of how during the Noriega years Julio's sainted mother protested with women from other important Panamanian families. Tell about how these women stood day after day in the shade of a spreading Cieba tree in condemnation of the misuse of power by the pockmarked general whom they called El Sapo—the toad. Explain that when the general caused the ancient tree under which they sheltered to be cut down, the women erected a canvas shelter and continued to gather each day to stare curses up at the windows of his residence.

For a moment I even consider revealing to my well meaning aunties and uncles that Julio's family is dead set against our union. They believe he is ordained for politics in his country. Dating a gringa is accepted as a part of sowing his oats, marrying me will doom his prospects in Panamanian politics.

Julio and I have spend many hours talking of all this. Admittedly these hours are woven into and around love making but nonetheless, I understand what his choosing me means to him and to his family. Every discussion about our future is webbed with the knowledge of that sacrifice. His unwillingness to walk away from me, his push toward a deeper commitment, is based in part on his desire to abandon his family's political ambitions for him and instead pursue his own dream, which is to develop real estate in both his country and around the world. His dream of independence is thus directly tied to his relationship with me.

But I say none of that to my family, instead I smile like a person who has her life under control, take their concern that I might be dating a member of a drug cartel as coming from love, and say only, "No Latin Mafia connections Uncle. Just a legitimate family business."

I could leave it at that. I should probably leave it at that. I can't leave it at that. I open my mouth and ask Uncle Jackie, "Why? Were you thinking of exporting some of your home grown?"

Aunt Enid gives a little yelp of laughter, Uncle Walter snorts beer up his nose and Uncle Jackie fusses at me, "Now Goo Goo you know them there plants is medicinal. For my glaucoma. You know that girl."

The fingernail moon isn't up yet when I slip my arm through Uncle Walter's and we walk out under the pines. Most of the uncles and aunties have already gone home. Samuel Martin has just pulled in with the Foster twins from across the county line, over in Dothan. The girls are two years younger and a decade more experienced than me. In a county of mostly long legged redheads and blondes, their butt length shiny black hair and Dolly Parton bodies are a wet dream novelty. I want to talk to Samuel, but I'll wait till the testosterone dust settles a bit.

All us cousins to the 'enth degree grew up together. Aunt Enid has a picture taken at Great grandpa Barr's eighteenth birthday party, the one where we all recited General Lee's ode to the great Traveller. The photo shows sixty four cousins spread in this very park. A good many are standing with their arms around each other's necks. Some are holding a younger cousin on a hip, three are holding up fingers like devil horns behind the head of the unsuspecting cousin in front of them. Samuel and I are standing next to each other, but he is a part of the lopsided triangle and I am a few feet outside the group looking away from the camera.

I have always thought that photo was an accurate picture of my teen years. I was always, by choice, on the outskirts of the group of cousins, a loner in the company of extroverts. I spent far more time growing up with my older uncles and aunts than with my cousins. At the time I didn't think anything about it, I only knew that I preferred the quiet company of Uncles Walter or Earl or Neil over the boisterousness of kids my age. In retrospect I suppose losing my mama and daddy probably caused me to seek shelter and approval. My good fortune was in having a plentitude of good and honorable uncles and loving aunts to take up the slack. Without those good men and women I might have turned out more like yonder Foster twins.

It's full dark, a curve of moon just rising above Hunley Ridge as Uncle Walter and I walk to the edge of the piney woods.

"The fireflies are already gone for the year," his low voice comes to me in the dark, "The deer'll be coming down the mountain looking to escape them colder nights."

I tell him about the lantern flies in Panama. "Uncle Walter, they were so big that the first night I saw them in the jungle around my house I imagined myself surrounded by painted Embera Indians clutching tiny flashlights."

Uncle and I make plans to track down a buck he's been watching up on the backside of Martin's ridge. It's a week before hunting season, but we aren't going to be doing anything but sighting down a long barrel and counting coup.

"He's a big'un." Uncle tells me, "Five or six pointer and heavy. Front left leg turns out just a tad with an old split in the hoof."

"He's a big'un." Uncle tells me, "Five or six pointer and heavy. Front left leg turns out just a tad with an old split in the hoof."

We have our backs to the party; stand side by side looking into the dark of the woods. I've left Julio in the company of Uncles Earl and Neil, the three of them planning a gator hunt in Panama's Lake Gatun.

My eyes have adjusted to the dark so that I can make out the old stump where Uncle Walter sat and whittled me a primitive recorder when I was eight. Tonight our respect for red ants keeps us from lowering ourselves onto the convenient seat. We look into the silent trees, both of us knowing we need to work out an agreement about Julio, neither of us quite sure how to do that and afraid words will only make the tension between us worse.

"I know he's not who you would have chosen for me," I finally say into the night, "but I'm asking you to believe that I've not forgotten a single thing you've taught me about what's important."

Behind us someone has set up speakers and Montgomery Gentry are shaking the remaining leaves from the maples, the bass a buzz of vibration running along my spine. I pick up auditory scraps of the rock of Big and Rich, Toby Keith's growl, and a female voice I recognize as Miranda Lambert wailing about gunpowder and lead while my fervent prayers go unanswered. When the silence has built to a cold hard wall between us, Uncle Walter touches my shoulder lightly before he walks to his truck, calls back over his shoulder that he'll pick me up Tuesday just before dawn to go tracking.

Chapter Six

Once Uncle Walter disappears into the night, I turn around so that I'm looking at what remains of the lantern lit welcome party. My tears blur the scene some, making wavy lines and fuzzy images of my remaining cousins. Twenty yards to my left I hear what can only be the drunken wandering of a couple of rednecks looking for a place to piss in the woods. Male bonding good ole boy style. As I start back to join the crowd, I hear the sound of urine splashing on pine needles.

The slur carries to me across the night.

"Nigger loving bitch ought to be taught a lesson is what I'm sayin'."

"All them Barrs is too high and mighty fer they own good."

In a strange way these words are a blessing to me. Angry at Uncle Walter's silent treatment, I'm stymied as to how to combat his disapproval. But this here, this outright bigoted trash, this here I know how to handle.

This is Cousin Mason and that half-wit Wally Watson. I've been dealing with these two loud mouths since first grade when the two of them cornered me in the school yard and attempted to yank my pony tail down and my dress up. That little scar that cuts through Mason's eyebrow, that's been there since the aforementioned little incident in grade school.

Tonight my anger pushes my legs forward with no thought whatsoever. The boys are still splattering recycled

Jax onto the floor of the woods when I slide up behind them and tap them both on the shoulder.

"Hey! You got something you want to say to my face?"

The idiots turn into each other as they circle to face me. I, not being drunk, step back much quicker than these two. They piss all over each other for a full four seconds before their inebriated brains catch on to what's happening.

"Holy shit Goo Goo," Mason slurs as he tucks himself away. "What the hell girl. You scared the bejesus outa me."

Wally is slower to respond. He stands peering into the darkness with that little bitty thang in his hand.

The two of them are mere shadows in the woods. I've moved off to the left of them, stand still, keeping quiet. I let them wonder where I am for a minute or two, allow their beer soaked brains to remember all the times growing up when they have been taught that it simply does not do to piss off a redneck girl.

They shift their feet a time or two.

"Y'all don't scare us none girl!" Wally lies into the dark.

I let 'em stew until they build up their courage and start back toward the crowd. Then I follow along behind, call out just as they step into the yellow light of the hanging lanterns, "Nice night for a walk in the woods, eh boys?"

It's cousin Gerald's voice I hear next.

"Lordy Mason, Wally, whaddit y'all do? Have yourselves a little pissing contest did ya?"

Like deer in the headlights of an oncoming car filled with gun toting hillbillies, my two big talking cousins stand exposed, their splattered jeans clearly visible, sheepish looks on their faces.

Time to end this before it escalates any further. I step between the boys, put my arms around their shoulders.

"Did I hear you two say you wanted to buy me a beer?"

It's Mason whose eyes I stare into. Wally ain't never been anything but a tag along. Into Mason's ear I whisper like a lover, "You're entitled to your own opinion hoss. But if you got something to say to me, have the balls to say it to my face."

Things settle down quickly after that. There is not a soul there who doesn't know that cousin Mason has just attended a mandatory come to Jesus meeting. Now the thing to keep in mind is that a good many less vocal cousins are closer to Mason's philosophical view than they are to mine. This sends a ripple of tension through the night, but family is family and the surface of things smooth out rapidly. The party flows on. Lines have been drawn in the red dirt of southern Georgia. Sometimes the only way on this green earth to get respect is to instigate a smidgen of fear.

Watching my cousins two step to Chris LaRoe, I think about how I half expected Julio's appeal to wilt in the Georgia dirt like those hothouse orchids for which you pay a fortune and drag home from Home Depot only to find them already wilting and with brown spots on their pristine blooms before you can get them from the car to the house. Instead, removed from among all the other exotics and surrounded by metaphorical zinnias and dog woods and magnolias, the man's appeal has heightened. My feelings for him deepen even as the sharp stone of Uncle Walter's anger and disappointment gnaw in my gut, the hurt in Uncle's eyes clarifying what Mason and Wally have just demonstrated. Bringing Julio back to Noisy Creek has changed me forever in the eyes of people I love and respect.

Disapproval of an extraordinarily handsome man with manners and money, who treats me like the princess I was raised to be, well, there's a historical context that is difficult to explain to anyone not from around here. Difficult because its basis resides not so much in our heads as in our fears, in the core of who we are as a people. In Noisy Creek, you see, there are white folks and then there is everybody else. What most of the world would label as Asian or Latin or Indian, my kinfolk just lumps together in one big mess they call colored. I'm not telling you it makes any sense. I'm not defending it as intelligent or even as rational. I'm just explaining to y'all how things are.

Now it's no longer a secret that a few southern white men have crossed race lines sexually since the first boatload of slaves arrived from Africa. But that's culturally different from a white woman having sex with a dark man. Different because wives get pregnant with babies their husbands then help to raise. More importantly it's different because the virtue of the south resides with its women. Different also because northern liberals have been attempting to overshadow the southern white man's culture since the occupation they called reconstruction. That line I mentioned is not so much in the sand as carved deep into core of the southland. Bringing Julio home, I've crossed it.

The only reason I'm still standing is that Julio isn't black, he's Latin. So I've fudged the line a little, tried to slip one past my vigilant uncle. That my lover is lighter skinned than many of my dark haired uncles and cousins, that he is highly educated, with more money than most of us, all of this matters intellectually, of course it does. But it doesn't change their visceral, gut level reaction that a nigger has got his hands on their pale skinned princess. Now I understand that there are folks to whom that attitude is offensive. Well, frankly, there is just nothing on God's green earth I can do about that. Offense doesn't change cultural reality. Everyone is a bigot of one kind or another. We all carry our peculiar prejudices and irrational beliefs. It has been my experience that the more irrational the belief the stronger and deeper it's roots run down into our murky core.

None of this knowledge changes the fact that, in bringing Julio home I have covered myself with an everlasting stain that no amount of logic or time is ever going to wash clean. I AM from around here. I know how things work. I remember clearly the long ago moment when I understood that irreparable damage could be incurred based on who a person chose to love.

I raised an Angus calf as my 4-H project when I was ten. I made the state finals and a whole troop of us carried that calf in a wobbly horse trailer all the way to Atlanta for the competition. Dark Chocolate Barr was eliminated at the first round giving me and the aunties and uncles plenty of time to wander the fair grounds. What I remember most about that day isn't leading Dark Chocolate from the ring as a loser, it's not the near blinding heat or the smells of hotdogs and cotton candy and hot grease. The moment that sticks in my head happened outside the poultry barn—a young man so black he looked purple in the direct sun hugging on a young blonde woman in cut off jeans whose skin was white enough that I could see the blue veins just below the surface on the backs of her dimpled thighs.

It was striking that scene. Visually the contrast was arresting, almost shocking and I might have carried only that remembrance except that Aunt Enid had gasped when she saw the two young people, instinctively jerked at my hand to lead me on a wide path around the scene as though the two were infectious carriers of incurable contagion. Her words confirmed what her body language had already communicated.

"I know that there mixing is right common up he-ah in the city but Honey, when they break away, there's gonna be some a that black has rubbed off on that gal."

Nobody had to tell me that it would be a permanent stain.

The stars are close under a thin crescent moon hanging so low it looks hung in the black branches of the magnolias that rim Travellers Park. With the older folks gone home, I teach Julio the Country Swing and the Texas two step. He attempts to dance the tango to the beat of Merle and Toby and Patsy. His request for a slightly different genre of music brings forth laughter and the proclamation from Cousin Larry that, "We got both kinds a music. We got Country and we got Western."

Just having returned from eighteen months of a constant diet of salsa and reggae, I don't feel one bit sorry for the man. I do not turn loose of his arm either. A good number of my girl cousins, as well as the Foster twins, appear to be contemplating rubbing up against my man to see if some of that exotic stain might not rub off. On the dance floor, or in this case in the red dirt, the man moves like a light breeze through tall trees. Dancing with Julio is the softest, longest, best foreplay imaginable.

"In my country is fiesta tradition to dance with many people. Is the same here, yes?" he asks as The Twins from Horniville make a beeline for my honey.

"No. Not at all. Here it is considered in very bad taste to dance with anyone but the one that brung ya."

I swear this with a straight face, turn him to me, kiss him a little fiercely.

When we break apart, he rubs the back of my neck, "I am thinking," he says as he brings his hands around until they are tipping my chin toward him, "you are a very bad liar and a very good kisser."

"Is this a combination you find appealing?" I ask, my breath already catching in my throat.

"So far, so well."

"So far, so good," I correct, though he is communicating magnificently.

I have spent a few sleepless hours in the last month listening to the high pitched craka craka of tree frogs and sweating in the Panamanian heat wondering how I'd feel when I saw Samuel Martin. He was my first kiss, my first lover, my best friend through four years of high school. More than that though, he was the boy my family expected me to marry. For four years all of Noisy Creek, myself included, thought of him as the future father of my children, the man with whom I'd grow old.

By the time I finally get to talk to Samuel just after midnight, I've been watching him surreptitiously for hours as he stalks The Twins and pretends to ignore me. He finally makes his way over to sit beside Julio and me on a plaid blanket smelling slightly of horse sweat that someone has thrown down and which I commandeered a moment before. The two men are a little like stiff legged dogs circling a bitch but they put a good veneer on it and speak politely about the ball game earlier in which they were on opposing teams. Julio gets up from the blanket in one of those fluid easy movements of his that always makes me think of long, smooth muscles and a dozen or so ways I'll put that agility to good use once I get him alone.

"I leave you to talk," he says in a gracious tone of voice that proclaims his confidence like a trumpet blast. "Your cousin Yolanda? With this one I may dance?"

His smile matches the sparkle in his eyes. Cousin Yolanda is what we call big boned. Close to three hundred pounds of plus size. Clearly the man is telling me that he is not in the least threatened by my past with Samuel, while I, jealous twit that I am, am so unsure of myself that I have kept him on a short leash all night. I'm hoping my smile conveys to him my pleasure in his accurate assessment of the situation.

"You've stirred things up around here," Samuel says as we watch Julio twirl a blushing Yolanda to the twang of a steel guitar.

I don't want to discuss Julio with Samuel.

"You tell your mama and them yet that y'all are going to Arkansas instead of up to Athens for that engineering degree?"

"I'm tryin' to remember," Samuel drawls, "in all the years we went together, did I ever win an argument with you?"

The two of us have kept in touch with email and the occasional letter, but we haven't seen each other or, I realize as I listen to his deep bass, heard the sound of each other's voices for almost four years. I've grown used to Julio's lilting baritone, forgotten completely how that low growl in Samuel's voice vibrates something deep in the area of my pelvis.

I clear my throat, shift my legs so my twanging parts are pointing away from Samuel Martin. I remind myself that, as the good ole boy he is, Samuel's idea of foreplay was the equivalent of, "Get in the truck girl." Still an image jumps into my head, though perhaps a little lower is actually the headwaters of the image.

Samuel and I are on a blanket in the bed of his pickup, a beacon of summer stars overhead, the smells of home all around. He is telling me about the house he'll build us down in that hollow where his great-great granddaddy Robert had his still. This image of the two of us is so strong it's as if I've been transported, like in one of those Star Trek episodes Samuel always loved, back to that warm summer night with the smell of rain in the air. I remember, re-experience is closer to the truth, those four tiny freckles on Samuel's belly that make a near perfect box around that line of pale blond hair that disappeared into the V of curls where my mouth had just been.

"Let's walk some," I say, suddenly in desperate need of movement, some way to exorcise these traitorous little sparks of psychic energy.

I lead us to edge of the dance floor where Julio, with his usual grace and charming smile, is dipping Yolanda in a rotator cuff tearing movement known as the chicken wing.

"Remember when Cooter tore his shoulder doing that there same move with some ole gal claimed to be kin to Jimmy Carter?" Samuel asks and we both laugh remembering that warm jasmine thick night of dancing and youthful lies.

Now, watching Julio twirl Yolanda in the packed red dirt of Travellers park, Samuel and I grin conspiratorially at each other, our shared history like a faded pair of jeans. Even though I know they're not going to fit any more no matter how I wiggle and suck in my breath, I just can't help but stroke em a bit, remembering old times. I reach across and squeeze his hand

This reminiscing about old days is interesting but right now from where I'm standing it appears that my tramp stamped Cousin Lizzie has one of her slut pink fingernails on my man's beautiful ass. I drag Samuel onto the dance floor where, through no fault of my own, one of my elbows happens to accidentally ram into the exposed belly of Cousin Lizzie.

Chapter Seven

The light is a lavender tinted halo around our heads. Wedged between Aunt Ruth and Uncle Walter, Julio and I are in the Barr Pew of the Central Babtist church. Cousin Lizzie is two rows back in the Ragsdale pew. I pray that gal is opening her heart to Jesus this early Sunday morning. The look she shot me as we came down the aisle to take our place under the stain glass window of Jesus letting the little children come unto him, well it was most un-Christian that glare. Downright ugly is what it was.

I am sorry I made a bruise on her perfect little body, but frankly it's not like she hasn't already marked herself up with that tattooed field of butterflies leading the way to the crack in her oversized ass.

The two of us have been scrapping since she tried to poke out my eyes when she was a spoiled one year old and I was a tiny helpless newborn. She stole my pink bicycle with the glitter honking horn when I was six and I retaliated by throwing rocks at her until I backed her up into a field of poison sumac.

You'd think we'd get along better. We're first cousins for the love of Jesus. She's my mama's sister's girl. We might have worked things out as we got older but when I was twelve, she stole Lester Calhoun Goodin. Lester may not have been the brightest in the class but he was the best looking boy in Noisy Creek. He's still as beautiful as a new colt in an alfalfa field, but being married to Yolinda Foster, who has managed to give birth to a set of twins every year now since high school, that there has dulled him some around the edges.

But in seventh grade that boy was a joy to behold. He walked me to and from school each day and the two of us shared our fried baloney sandwiches and cold wedges of pie at our own special place at a scarred Formica cafeteria table. Now I admit, even at the age of eleven, I knew my attraction to Lester was based solely on his good looks. The boy could only talk about football and was downright lethal as a partner in science lab. Before Cousin Lizzie Ragsdale sat herself down at our table and proceeded to work her wiles on the unsuspecting and naive boy, I had about decided to branch out some in my choice of friends.

Once Lizzie stepped into the picture though, Lester was magically transformed into something valuable and worth fighting for. Though that little altercation didn't last long. Cousin Lizzie cheated, but she quickly won. I don't like to speak ill of relatives but let's just say that as early as junior high Cousin Lizzie had carpal tunnel problems which escalated after each out of town game when, as a majorette, she rode the bus with the football team. A shared baloney sandwich isn't much competition against that kind of deal. Lester quickly recanted his undying love for me and I returned to eating lunch at the edge of my cousins.

This became a pattern. If I liked a boy, well then Lizzie adored him and had a truly magical experience she was delighted to share with him. Until Samuel came along. I believe that one of the reasons I fell in love with him was that he was immune to Cousin Lizzie. Even before the two of us invented our own special magic, that boy found Lizzie Ragsdale positively repulsive. Or pretended to. Either way, I loved him for it.

Now, I admit, none of this history excuses my behavior last night. I actually have been raised better than to plant a pointy elbow into the belly of a man stealing scank, but when I looked out there and saw those poutie lips pointed at my Julio, that dirty little expert hand on his gorgeous ass, well I behaved like the redneck woman I am. As we stand and raise our voices in praise and adoration with 'The Old Rugged Cross', I'm thinking that elbow was probably a mistake.

I should have belted the bitch.

After church we follow Aunt Ruth and Collin out to their new home at the back side of Green Acres. I have discovered that Julio never learned to drive a stick shift. This knowledge inspires in me a need to pop gears causing the old transmission to scream like a scalded cat and Julio to grip the oh shit bar until his knuckles are white as a frog's belly. I eventually take pity on him sitting there watching the road rush by through the dinner plate sized hole in the floor boards at his feet and ease up.

My reduced speed has as much to do with the truck's need of realignment as it does with concern for Julio's fear. That and I may have just seen a piece of the side panel fly off into the piney woods as I made that last curve coming around the Cemetery at the Church of God. Up ahead I see Aunt Ruth slow down to accommodate my reduced speed.

"We follow your aunt?" Julio asks, "or chase? Is different these two words yes?"

"Not in Noisy Creek it ain't," I confirm for him.

"Before you have the fist fight with your cousin with who I am having a nice dance, did you have a good talk with your Samuel Martin?"

I reach across the seat and put my hand on his thigh. He quickly places my hand back on the vibrating steering wheel, not so much a rejection as a will for survival.

We didn't get back to the house on Clanton Lane last night until just a few hours before dawn. Both of us had been filled with a need to own the other sexually. A need that wasn't completely satisfied until minutes before we were required to rise from bed to get ready for church. My feeling today is that, while we haven't talked about Cousin Lizzie or discussed Samuel Martin, we've already communicated their irrelevance to our relationship. Julio however, isn't finished with the topic.

I turn the pick-up off route 4 and up a dirt road along the north side of Martins Ridge. About a quarter mile up is a spot wide enough to pull the old truck up under the pines where it rattles and shakes for a full minute after I've removed the key. I step out into the tang of a pine forest. Coming around to Julio's side of the truck, it occurs to me that already I have no clear memory of the smells of the jungle. In Panama I often woke with this smell right here in my head. Even now when it's weeks too late for the blooms, I can smell the honeysuckle and jasmine mixing with the tang of pine and the rich smell of red dirt.

Julio steps out into the tall grass, the door of the truck banging ineffectively against the bent frame. He's forgotten to lift and push. I take his hand and lead him through the brown pine needles, around a Sweetgum stump softened with the insidious green leaves of kudzu, and out into a small meadow. I am struck again with the notion that I only breathe fully when it's this home-tinged air that I'm drawing down into my lungs.

There's a chunk of limestone just at the edge of the meadow, its top worn smooth by a millennium of Georgia wind and rain. We sit on this natural bench, our thighs touching, my head on Julio's shoulder. The sky is a streaked gray masterpiece. Indigo blues and palest lavender overlaid whisper thin to make luminous pearly grays. The hunger for my camera, the need to capture the moment, stirs in me, though I know that the moment captured would be, as always, the moment past.

Movement in the tall grass to the left of us is a cotton tail making a meal of the tender clover that grows in the shade of an ancient oak.

"You have come here with Samuel?" Julio asks and, finally, I understand why he needs to talk.

In Panama he shared me only with his country's moths and butterflies. In Panama I am Georgia Ginny Barr, entomologist and part time photographer, girl-friend of Julio Hernandez Monterey. Here in Noisy Creek, I am Goo Goo Bar, orphaned child, shy adolescent, old lover and friend, much loved niece and competitive cousin. The realization that home layers me in these veils of moments past makes my breath catch in my throat, confirms what I have risked by bringing Julio here. The nine year old child who sits alone in the dark quakes in fear. I swing around so that I'm straddling Julio's waist, lower myself onto his lap, face to face with my chosen future.

We sit like this until the warmth of our bodies has stilled my shivering, no more or less than a part of the woods around us. A cool breeze carries the whistle of a deer making its way through the woods on the other side of the meadow. I know the deer will be walking on thin legs, can picture her stopping to taste the air, watchful of cougar or poaching redneck. It takes me a long time to move dream slow from Julio's lap to my place beside him looking out into the meadow, but I still beat the doe's appearance. The white flick of the underside of a tail gives away her presence moments after I've turned my face toward her. When she steps out from the shadows of the pine trees, I hear Julio draw in his breath, feel his body tense against mine.

I constantly forget that I have fallen in love with a city boy. I give him the line he gives me when I worry about Panama City traffic or the paperwork of immigration in his country.

"No problem," I whisper as the doe raises her head, pulls her ears forward toward the sound.

Her caution tells me she has a fawn or two with her, still hidden in the dark of the woods at her back. I have been here to this meadow with Samuel, but mostly, I have been here with Uncle Walter. For years an old buck owned these woods. There were usually three or four does and his sons and daughters roaming the area as well, but the buck is who Uncle and I tracked. I had him in my sites as a forked horn, never got close to him the next year or the year after, but found him again as a four pointer the year before I left for college. That buck can't still be alive, has probably provided a meal for the cougar family that has its den up in the rocks above Snow Camp, but one of his sons may still be in possession of the mountain.

The grass is so tall that the only way I know the fawns have moved out from under the trees at the doe's whistling call is the movement of the seed heads at the surface of the meadow. The ringing of my cell phone startles me almost as much as the doe. I jump an instant before she startles and leaps across the meadow snorting for her young to follow. Only now do we catch a glimpse of the fawns as the three dear disappear back into the dark of the woods. Cursing myself for not remembering to turn off the cell phone, I pick up to hear Aunt Ruth telling me they'll be eating dinner in an hour and to warn me that Uncle Walter is in a black mood. Aunt Snickers and her new beau Preston Yates are coming as well.

"Sorry I didn't call," I tell Aunt Ruth, "We stopped at Hunley Ridge for a minute."

"That's fine Honey," Aunt Ruth says. "We haven't got started here yet. My word, but you were driving slow there just before I lost you. I was afraid y'all maybe had trouble with that old truck of your Uncle Earls, is why I called."

"Y'all have another piece a this here pie now," Great Aunt Selma says as she slips a wedge of peach pie onto Julio's plate next to a half eaten slice of pecan.

We are all of us as fat as ticks. Great Uncle Hershal Barr is already sitting in front of the TV in the living room with the top button of his pants undone. He'll be asleep by the time we finish our dessert. Uncles Earl and Neil are on the porch with a red and blue sack of Bugle, rolling papers and a cooler of Schiltz. The two of them are in cahoots with Julio and planning some fishing trip extraordinaire. They've been spinning him tales all afternoon about Appaloosa Catfish as big as Volkswagens, three hundred pound Gar Fish and the southern sport of Gator Wrestlin'.

I love him to death but this is a man who has never worn anything but custom tailored clothes, a man who can't even drive a stick shift, it is mighty difficult for me to picture him in a skiff with my two Dickie overall clad Uncles. Still I leave it alone, at least they're congenial toward him. My Uncle Walter on the other hand, has refused to say a word all day, making it clear that his attendance at this dinner is under duress.

Much of this afternoon's talk has been about the new Yatesville Project out on Martin's Ridge. From what I can gather the Bessie Smith Park was Aunt Snicker's idea, a sort of sop to the locals so as to avoid a lynching of her new boyfriend. This is my first time meeting the infamous Preston Yates. Tall and with thick shiny white hair and glowing teeth, he does seem marginally Great Satan-ish in a Rich Yankee Carpetbagger sort of way, but he also seems devoted to Aunt Snickers.

The grand opening of the park is set for the second week in October. The statue of Bessie Smith, hero of the mythical battle of Noisy Creek, will be unveiled and there is to be something called a Redneck Goddess Contest in which I have already been entered.

When I object to participating in any such contest, Aunt Snickers points out that Cousin Lizzie has already registered—as though this information can manipulate me into changing my mind. Still, it might be fun this contest. It does sound interesting. There's to be a hunting and fishing competition. Also some race that involves repairing a four wheel drive vehicle, driving it across a creek and then through an obstacle course set up along Martin's Ridge. There's a cooking contest with rules stating the contestant must grow or kill the major ingredients themselves. Last, but certainly not least, the beauty competition requires bare feet and denim.

It's a fact that the longer my ancestral psychic roots feed on the soil of Noisy Creek, the more my redneck nature flourishes. Coming in from the porch where I've partaken of a can or two of the contents of the uncle's cooler, I announce, "Hell yeah I'll participate in The Redneck Goddess Contest. If Cousin Lizzie wants to get her ass whipped I'm just the gal to do it. Yee haw! Just show me where to sign my name."

In my defense I rarely drink due to the fact that I generally get a bit carried away in my enthusiasms when I do so. In the past this tendency has led to a broken femur at eighteen when I jumped the gate and attempted to ride Uncle Warren's Hereford bull; a scary two weeks while I waited for my period after Samuel and I shared a flask of tequila; and, more recently, waking in a hammock to the sounds of howler monkeys, a thousand mosquito bites and a half empty bottle of Panama Jack Rum. So, all in all, I don't think signing up to be a contestant in The Redneck Goddess Contest is really all that remarkable.

Dusk is a rivulet of fire on a tarnished silver horizon. All day Uncle Walter's disapproval of my involvement with Julio has been an ache that not even the Shiltz can dull. His silence, which started as a pebble in the toe of my homecoming has now worn a bloody crippling blister. I'm starting to get pissed off. From the window over Aunt Ruth's kitchen sink I see him out under the spread of a White Hickory, the branches bare and dark against the paler sky. His back is to the house, his view the setting sun. I watch as he absently kicks at the hickory nuts that fell at first frost. It's time to apply soft words like mole skin in the hope of healing a relationship that is central to who I am. If that doesn't work I intend to verbally cut deep and quick and let the poison drain. Either way, I'm done limping along pretending each step isn't filling my boot with blood.

I walk up behind him, lift his arm and drape it around my shoulder. With the side of my head resting on his chest, the acrid smell of Winstons and honest sweat has me crying too soon for it to be based totally on Uncle's degree of pungency. All afternoon I've practiced what to say to convince him that my being with Julio is acceptable. When Julio commented on the number of young people in uniform among Aunt Ruth's collection of family photos, I waited for Uncle Walter to give his lecture on the honor of serving this great country. Could hear his tone and that tiny catch in his voice the subject always brings. But it was Uncle Earl who eventually cleared his throat and declared that when the U. S. of A calls, the south always provides more than its fair share of soldiers. Uncle Walter only made a noise like the clearing of a lifetime of phlegm from his throat and walked out to the porch for a smoke.

From the moment the door slammed behind him, my hurt became anger. All afternoon I've nursed that anger, even fed it a little beer. I've done my best to build up a righteous indignation which, when I left Aunt Ruth's kitchen a minute ago, I fully intended to let loose on my stubborn uncle. Now, with my face pressed against the soft blue flannel covering his chest, my throat is too tight to emit anything but squeaks I haven't heard since I was nine. I know that the aunts and uncles and my worried Julio watching from the house are seeing a grown women hugging the stiff neck of an old mule of a farmer. But what's really happening out here under this Hickory tree is a little girl whose just lost her mother is clinging to a man whose love will keep her grounded her whole life.

Through the stark black branches of the Hickory, the first distant stars are set in a velvet sky when I finally get control of my grief and fear.

I step away from Uncle Walter to wipe my face, clean myself up some. I grin at him across the half foot of night air separating us.

We stand silent for another little time. The kitchen light goes off and I relax a bit more into the protective darkness of home.

"Saw a doe and two fawns at Little Meadow."

I say it without the pronoun deliberately. Not 'We saw' or 'Julio and I saw'. Not yet.

Uncles Earl and Neil are arguing amiably on the back porch. The night air carries only an occasional growl or exclamation, but I don't need to hear the words to know they're still swapping fishing tales.

The thick night air blankets us softly. Uncle Walter tells me he found the head and antlers of the buck he and I tracked up on that ridge for years.

"Died natural I think, but an old mama black bear was feedin' on the carcass."

Black bear aren't common around here. I've never seen one in the wild though they're around. The summer I worked with Uncle Nuggie in his taxidermy shop, hunters from over in Clayton County brought one in. Watching Uncle skin that bear out was a fascinating thing to a twelve year old budding naturalist like myself. I'd skinned deer of course, but we were never particularly careful with the hide. It was the venison we were getting at, after all, not some trophy skin. Uncle Nuggie skinned the paws on the bear himself but he let me skin out the head. Skinless bears chased me through my dreams for a month afterward, but the anatomy was fascinating.

"Black bear ain't usually meat eaters," Uncle reminds me, but he warns, "this here one though, she's old, probably a female by her size and crippled up in her left shoulder if I'm reading her prints rightly. That mess up there on the ridge that your Aunt Snicker's paramour is up to, that is a heap a trouble for the local wildlife.

"That south side where they're puttin' in those log castles?" he asks and I nod my head where it rests against his chest, surprised and happy to hear this many words from my generally taciturn Uncle, "You recall it used to be all wild black berries over there. The berries are gone.

Replaced with Japanese Zen gardens and English mazes for all this ole hillbilly knows."

He slides around so we're standing face to face.

"That bear is hungry and I think she's probably in pain from that old injury. You be careful, you wander up on that ridge."

Even in the dark I can see the glint in Uncle's eyes as he adds, "Don't want that ole bear catchin' your Julio unawares. Be getting indigestion from that foreign food no doubt."

An almost gentle cuff on the shoulder accents my laughter before I catch up his hand and we leave the wet chill of the dark autumn night and head inside to join the rest of the family.

Chapter Eight

Layers of iron gray clouds merging with ghostly ground fog mute Monday morning's light. I peek out the front window first thing, pull aside the curtain and separate the blinds for a view of the front lawn. No burning cross. I take that as a fine start to the day.

I'm cradling the warmth of my first cup of coffee against my chest, the steam, rising slowly in the moist air when I step out the back door, is absorbed by the cold before it reaches my chin. In Panama the yellow head parrots will be screeching out their first welcome of the day; the Honeycreepers will be leaping among the hibiscus well into their morning gossip; right about now, as I enjoy my first sip of coffee here in the cool of Noisy Creek, the traffic in Panama City is already a symphony of honking horns. I smile over the top of my coffee cup, step quickly back inside and mutter to myself that, here in Noisy Creek, the morning is colder than a witch's tit.

I pulled Aunt Ruth's flowered duvet over Julio ten minutes ago and left him curled on his side sleeping peacefully. I want time to think this morning, to sort out my feelings about being home. It's not just my relatives who are finding me changed from when they last saw me. My image of myself is surprisingly different than I expected.

Silly but I thought that coming back to Noisy Creek would return me to being the girl I was seven years ago when I drove out of town in a battered Ford Escort on my way to Athens, Georgia for my first year of college. That I am no longer that eighteen year old whose whole world lie within the confines of Hunley Mountain and Martin's Ridge, well that has come as a surprise to me. Noisy Creek is now and always will be home. I still define myself as a small town southern redneck, still love being a Barr. But I am also now an entomologist and naturalist, a photographer and a lover of exotic light and a dark skinned man who ain't from around here.

This morning, watching a cardinal peck at the empty bird feeder, I'm reminded of Aunt Candy's favorite bible verse, the one that exhorts us to work out our own salvation in fear and trembling. There are moments, as this hybrid I have become, when I am comfortable in both worlds. Other times, I fear I will never belong to either world, never be accepted in Panama as anything but an eccentric gringa, forever now be seen in Noisy Creek only as the traiter that broke her Uncle's heart. In this maudlin mood, and with only a half cup of caffeine in my system, my mind finds another bible passage, the one that tells us that the son of man had nowhere to lie his head.

Julio's love feels like both a steady support and a stranglehold, depending on my mood at any given moment. My love for him is more straightforward—it scares me half to death. Call it fear of intimacy, call it chicken shit, call it what you will, I am a frightened child who both wants and fears the love this man is offering. I'm doing my very best to calm and reassure that unreasonable nine-year-old, but there are moments when I am right back in that graveyard watching the lowering of those pure white boxes. In those moments the need to feel Uncle's hand in mine is a hunger so deep that it's all I can do not to run to him and beg his forgiveness.

Time to stop contemplating and have that second cup of coffee, see what's in the fridge for breakfast and put bird seed on the grocery list. Julio and I have planned to spend the day together. Alone. I am going tracking with Uncle Walter before dawn tomorrow and Julio, my poor unsuspecting city boy, is going with Uncles Earl and Neil to some secret fishing hole whose location neither of them will reveal. I was teasing last night when I told him they were taking him to Dead Man's Cove and that today might well be our last day together, but there was a certain hard pellet of worry in my little joke.

I make a fresh pot of coffee, put the buttermilk biscuits, fried eggs and grits on the kitchen table and call down the hall to Julio who I heard stirring in there ten minutes ago. He comes out in just his pants, his flat belly and hard chest making me change my mind about breakfast being the most important meal of the day. He catches my look, pauses for a split second, gives me a chance to let the eggs get cold.

"Eat first," I say and give him a wink that promises morning delight for dessert.

Over breakfast I ask him how he's doing among my relatives so far. He takes a long time to answer. Picks a piece of egg out of his grits and pops it in his mouth. Butters a biscuit and smears it with peach blossom honey.

"The eggs and the fat white breads I like very much," he tells me solemnly, "the grits I do not care for."

"Biscuits," I tell him, "they're called biscuits. Grits are an acquired taste."

"Yes," he smiles at me as he enjoys his honey dripping fat white bread, "is the same with your relatives, no?"

"Have another little bite of grits. Try them with the eggs. The flavor will grow on you."

"I have better idea," he says as he takes my hand.

Turns out his idea does beat grits all to heck.

Aunt Ruth has taken pity on Julio and lent us her Volvo. It has an automatic transmission, intact floorboards and the steering wheel doesn't shimmy like the Georgia sun on a fast running creek. We park and walk through the pasture between Green Acres and Uncle Clark and Aunt Selma's place and head for the swimming hole. Julio is fascinated with the bales of hay that dot the land like round basket boats in a sea of fog. I am layering the moment with a hundred summer days, am surrounded by ghosts with lemonade breath and bony skinned knees, deafened by excited squeals and the songs of long grown cousins.

I don't remember when I learned to swim. The family story is that I fell in the creek when I was barely a toddler and scared my mama half to death by dog paddling with my head under water until Uncle Walter waded out to lift me up out of the water. My hair was just as fiery red then as it is now, and Aunt Ruth always tells the story that I looked like a tiny bedraggled Irish setter pup when Uncle pulled me into the air. Evidently I arched my back, screamed bloody murder until I was redeposited into the cool water. I suspect this story has been edited a bit, but it does seem to me that I was born loving this creek.

After Mama and Daddy died I came here almost every afternoon. I sat for hours on a flat chunk of dark granite in the speckled cool of the creek. Sprawled on that sun hot rock, watching the dragon flies buzzing vermillion and iridescent blue and gold over the leaf dappled creek, I was comforted. My grief was soothed by the occasional ka-ploob of a frog leaping from the muddy bank to bury itself in the slippery creek bottom, or the distinctive slap of a trout's belly on the surface of the water after leaping for one of the thousand gnats or black flies that swarmed in a rowdy ball in the shade of the overhanging Maple.

Years later, when I was in high school, I heard Pastor Coleman give a sermon—this was in early October just at the beginning of dear season he gave this little talk—in which he reminded us Baptist backsliders that we were not like the heathen who worshipped inanimate trees and even solid rock. His point, I suppose, was that all us rednecks ought to be in church listening to his words of wisdom instead of wandering around out in the woods looking for Bambi and spending our money on beer and bullets. I stopped listening when he described the trees and woods and rocks and dirt and sky as inanimate. For me, nothing could be further from the truth.

Which is why, as Julio and I slip and slide our way down the creek bank, I feel like I'm visiting old friends. More than that, I'm reuniting with a part of myself. The creek's running high and red, loud as it parts around the granite table in its center. I lead Julio to a thick bare branch of the red maple that hangs out over the swirling water. In summer smaller kids slide from here into the pool below, working up their courage to join their bigger cousins as they swing out on the ragged rope still dangling from a higher limb. Riding that hemp swing on its wide arch to the deepest spot in the swimming hole is so much a part of my childhood that, even now, I wake from dreams suspended in the moment between letting go of the rope and splashing into the gnat clouded waters of home.

Julio follows my lead as I scoot my behind along that maple limb before dropping down onto the granite bench. Orangey-red water eats at the edges of our perch, the smell of ancient alluvial mud rises up, engulfs us. We lower ourselves so that we're sitting with our booted feet dangling inches from the frothy water. I hold Julio's warm hand and listen to the old hymn that is the music of the creek. The air is soft with mist rising from the swirling eddies and joining with a soft rain that I know will turn to tiny sharp knives of cold within the hour. Julio reaches his arm around my back and draws me tighter against his side.

We sit like this a good long, peaceful time.

Protected in our verdant green ceilinged cathedral, the sky blocked from sight, we can't see the dark clouds that I know are rolling in from the southwest. But we can hear the thunder, far away and of seemingly no importance to the two of us.

"Do you think we can do this thing? You and me. Your family and mine?" I ask softly.

A flock of wild turkeys is moving down the creek bank. I glimpse the ridge of purple and maroon comb on the cock, haven't yet spotted the hens, but they're here. The cock is moving too slowly, too carefully to be alone. He's waiting for his ladies to take their time joining him for a muddy breakfast drink. I point the movement out to Julio and his squinting stare makes me grin. Just to the left of us, not ten feet from where we sit with our legs dangling off the boulder, is a shallow pool made by a jammed cedar tree. Bits of leaves and smaller branches have added to this dam to make a drinking hole for the creatures that live in this small patch of woods.

The delicate V tracks of a small doe and her fawns are there at the edge of the pool. It looks like Uncle Clark's hounds have been drinking here as well. I see where one slipped and slid down into the water in his enthusiasm for a drink or maybe he was chasing the cotton tail whose prints are just visible in the soft mud.

The turkey cock has stepped out now onto the flat red mud of the cove. He turns his head on his long neck, stares directly at us with his yellowy-brown eyes. Then, either because he judges us to not be a threat, or simply because he doesn't see us as we sit holding our breath, he gives a clicking signal and four fat hens move down the bank and join him for a drink.

Julio and I watch this little wildlife tableau until the turkeys finish their drink and disappear back into the woods.

"I think," I tell Julio, "we might be eating that big guy for Thanksgiving dinner. That bird is nowhere near cautious enough to survive the holiday season living this close to my uncles."

With my words, Julio startles a little against me. Because he's not used to seeing living animals as potential food? Or because he's not planning on being here for the holidays? When I ask him this, his laughter rolls out over the water drowning out even the roar of the creek.

"My mother, she is speaking of coming here," he says into the wet air.

Now I'm the one who startles.

"Here? To Noisy Creek? Why would she do that?" This comes out in a high and decidedly squeaky voice. As though I've been goosed.

Julio's dark eyes sparkle with mischief but there is a hint of fear there too, as he tells me that, before we ever left Panama, he told his sainted mother that he loved me. That he would like to spend the rest of his life with the red haired gringa.

"My mother she would like now to meet your family," he says.

I remember to shut my mouth before any flies get in. I'm hearing the words 'rest of his life' over and over on a loop in my head while an image of my relatives dancing naked around his arrogant mother burns itself into my brain. Funny how easily shock and fear can send the mind catapulting into the abyss.

"This place you bring me, here," he asks gently, "this is your favorite place?"

His words make me jump like I've been touched with a live electrical wire. This morning, just before our second rising from bed, tangled with him in sex induced bliss, a thought like an epiphany had created an extra glow. This is my favorite place, I had thought, right here in this man's arms.

Right now the same man's arms are making me feel positively claustrophobic. I stutter and stammer. I actually think this a not a good time to have this conversation. I'm pretty sure I'm coming down with something. Some really virulent strain of flu is making me cold and clammy at the same time sweat is rolling down the small of my back.

A memory washes over me of Uncle Walter's low bass drawl the morning of my first debate team meet, when I woke sick. Just like this—cold and hot at the same time, shaky and teary and angry all at the same time. Chickenitis. That's what he said I had. Very common he told me. Only cure is to ignore it and get on with the things you want and need to do in this life.

I take a deep breath or ten. Release my strangle hold on Julio and watch the blood flow back into his hand. Force myself to drop my shoulders so they no longer nudge against my ear lobes. Make myself look honestly at the man sitting beside me on this dirty rock in his tailored clothing. Finally, I take one last gasping breath, like a heart attack victim whose just been brought back to life with those shock paddles and is surprised to find herself back in her body.

I tell him the truth. "With you here with me. Yes. I think this is my favorite place in the world."

"I love you very much. Georgia Jinny Goo Goo Bar," he says, now and I can feel my soul trying to fly away into the trees again. I'm holding on here by a thinnest thread of courage. But I'm holding on.

"I love you," I repeat back to him and the now knowledge that this is true is a splitting apart in my chest a red hot poker descending into dry ice, hope and fear combined.

"I think to do this someplace more elegant. A restaurant with the candles and the silver. But, I think now for you, this is the best place."

If I could move I would stop him. I think I would stop him.

From the pocket of his hand tailored wool coat, he takes an unmistakable navy blue velvet box. My hands, muddy from scooting along the branch overhanging the creek, are icy cold and a teeny bit twitchy as I push them deep into the pockets of my coat. The rain begins now in earnest, the frogs start their chorus of joyful welcome, and Julio lips open Pandora's box and I'm looking at an expensive very beautiful offering of love.

I see that William and I are in love I do. But any girl it is remembering the weekend I was fourteen and helped Uncle Bobby and Aunt Laurie castrate and brand their small herd of Herefords before turning them out on forest service land for winter grazing. I'm looking at a perfect two carat fire white diamond being offered by a gorgeous, loving man who I adore and I'm seeing a brand burning into the hind end of a calf.

The rain in tiny razors of cold on our faces. Julio slips off his jacket and drapes it over our heads, a soft woolen tent of security. The ring, still in its blue velvet nest, is a magnet in his hand, drawing my eyes down into its sparkling depths as if it were a crystal ball and I have only to gaze into it deeply enough to foretell my future.

"I'm scared about half to death," I whisper, our heads touching under the silk lined coat.

If he had hesitated, I might have gotten away but his voice is in my ear almost before I've finished speaking.

"Yes," he whispers into my ear. "This I know. The fear it is a little bird hitting against the walls, wanting escape, no?"

I nod my head against his chest, take my hands from my pockets and wrap them around him.

"But the heart," his voice flows over me. "It is strong like the bull."

I lift my left hand to him, think to brush off the dirt and end by smearing red mud on both my hands and on his as well. The ring comes close to being lost in the creek with the shaking of our hands, but we get it on my finger just as the hard rain turns to hail that bites at our legs.

We stay right there under his coat, our bodies the only warmth, while I cry until an attack of the hiccups causes me to fear we'll end up in the water if we don't move away from this rising creek. Later, I know I will swear the tears were of joy. And they are. They really are. But I am a child of parents who abandoned me to the love of my big, rowdy, opinionated family. Over the years I'll reframe the moment to focus on the joy, of course I will, but right now with stinging hail bouncing off our faces and into the waters of the creek, I know damn good and well that some of these tears are plain ole terror at what I am risking by joining my life with Julio.

Chapter Nine

By dawn we are in the woods. The sky is gun metal gray, the horizon streaked with the merest hint of orange when we start our slow careful climb up the north face of Martin's Ridge. I called Uncle Walter last night to tell him of my engagement. I knew the news would spread by cell phone, smoke signal and holler to every living soul in the county roughly two and half minutes after that ring slid on my trembling finger. We wanted to go to the house and tell Uncle Walter the news. Julio had some idea that he might work things out with Uncle if they could sit together mano a mano.

Uncle Walter wasn't having any of that.

"Tell me what you got to say Goo Goo," he growled at me over the phone when I asked if we might drop by. "You're the only person I need to hear things from."

When I told him Julio and I were engaged, the silence was so long that I thought he might have simply laid the phone on the scarred gray countertop there in the kitchen and walked away. I had time to relive a childhood of suppers sitting across the oak table from him, chattering about some bug I'd found that day, or going on about how Mary Lou Clark had up and cut off her waist length braid and shown up at school with her dark hair shorter than a boys. I had me plenty of time to ruminate on how Uncle always seemed genuinely interested in every little morsel of life that fell out of my mouth there as we sopped up our pot liquor with our cornbread and drank down our sweet tea.

Julio, who was watching me make the call from across the living room, had time to get up and come to me, wrap his arms around my shoulders, smooth down my wild curls and kiss the top of my head before I heard Uncle Walter's voice again.

"Four o'clock tomorrow morning is when I'll pick you up," is all he said before I heard the distinct click of a phone being carefully, deliberately, disconnected.

"Well," I told Julio when he asked what Uncle had said. "At least he and I going tracking tomorrow. So I guess he's still speaking to me."

We had come back to the house after our walk, wringing wet and shaking with cold and, for me at least, with some bit of shock at what we had done. An hour of sitting spooned in the old claw foot tub had left me limp and Julio less so. We spent the rest of the day in and out, mostly in, bed. Hiding under the covers from the cold and, I admit it, from the real world, many of whose inhabitants were going to be less than pleased at our news. I wanted a few hours of sexual bonding, whispered words, shared plans and dreams before exposing our happiness to the world outside the bedcovers.

After Uncle Walter, I called Aunt Ruth.

"Are you sure Goo Goo?" she asked. "You love him?"

When I assured her I did indeed love this man from a world as different from my own as cheese grits were from sancoche, the warmth and pleasure in her voice warmed me more fully than that earlier hour in her old claw foot tub. She asked to speak with Julio and, from the look on his face she was welcoming him to the family like the southern lady she is.

We saved The Sainted Mother for last. She didn't ask to speak with me or welcome me to the family. I decided to seat her next to Uncle Walter at the wedding reception. The two of them ought to find a wide field of common ground.

After the phone calls we ate every bit of the food in the refrigerator, all the fried chicken, green beans and collards, every bite of the biscuits and cornbread. We even finished off a half gallon of Bunny Tracks ice cream we found in the freezer. We didn't do this all at one sitting. We ate some. Made love some. Ate some more. Talked about where we'd live and how many children we wanted. Took ourselves to bed another time or two. We made plans and love until it was time to get ready for my tracking with Uncle Walter and Julio's fishing trip with Uncles Earl and Neil.

So, this morning, bouncing along beside Uncle Walter in his Chevy pickup after no sleep at all the night before, I gulp coffee from a stainless steel thermos and try not to take it personally when he refuses the extra cup I've brought for him. He hasn't said a single word, not so much as a grunt, all the way to the pull over at the base of the mountain. To my comment that the day looks like it's going to be clear and cold, he nods his head. Which I take as a positive and let it go.

Half way up the mountain, following a deer trail that leads around behind the meadow, a silent hour into this adventure, I'm starting to get a little pissed off.

Uncle Walter is packing his .30-06 but I have only my Olympus slung around my neck bouncing a little sore spot on my chest. I've grown unaccustomed to this cold.

My gloved hands are sheltered deep into the warmth of my armpits as we wind our way carefully up this shady side of the mountain. This is a whole lot more work than paddling around Panama's Lake Gatun as Blue Morpho butterflies as big as my hand flit over the brown waters and monkeys scream out their sunrise greeting.

At the edge of the meadow we hunker down and wait to see if the buck will come to us. I've logged days, maybe whole months if you add it all up, sitting next to Uncle Walter in companionable silence, listening to the sounds of south Georgia piney woods. A crow gave his squawking alarm when we settled ourselves an hour ago on a mossy log, half hidden behind a flowering quince. But solitary adult crows generally grow bored easily and this one was true to his nature and soon moved off in search of better entertainment. Before he could stop himself though Uncle Walter had grinned over at me when we heard the first piercing cry of that crow.

His name for me as a child was Red Crow. This was before my mama died when he was living in the back room and running the farm. I was more boisterous then I think, more apt to run to him with each new miracle I found under a rotten log or hidden in the branches of a tree. The day he nicknamed me Red Crow he was stringing wire fencing and being tormented in his work by a flock of the young black birds. Their cawing and squawking was bad enough but they had taken to dive bombing his head and when he objected they began swooping down and stealing the shiny hog nose rings he was using on the fencing. Already irritated by the crows, I interrupted his fencing work with a brown and orange salamander I found in the leaf litter at the edge of our water pump. Next came a millipede I dug out from under the porch. Followed by an empty sparrow's nest I'd skinned both elbows and one knee stealing from the branches of the sweet gum tree out behind the hen house, and then a lumpy baby toad I had imprisoned in a paper cup and wanted to keep as a pet. This was all before the noon meal. Uncle, in his exasperation, had finally proclaimed that I was worse than the crows for distracting a man from the joy of his work on a summer day.

This morning, as the cawing dies down and the silence settles over the woods, Uncle refuses to meet my eye, stares pointedly out over the meadow where the sun sprinkles a hundred spider webs with points of glittering silver. The need to reminisce with this stubborn man about this shared slice of my childhood is a wave building in my center, slapping against the levy of my anger. Just as the need to reconnect is beginning to overpower my anger, the call of a blue jay gives away the presence of something headed our way. A doe and two fawns are stepping through the high grass of the meadow on long elegant legs. I snap off a half dozen shots with the silent Olympus. The doe senses us watching her, remains on the far side of the clearing, keeps lifting her head and throwing her big ears forward.

If Uncle Walter and I hadn't been using so much of our energy being angry with each other, we might have caught on sooner. I like to think we would have. As it is, neither of us senses the bear until the wind changes. The doe whistles, leaps into the air and, her fawns right behind her, disappears into the woods. Then, and only then, do Uncle and I turn slowly around and look into the beady brown eyes of the bear. On a rock overhang about fifty feet behind us and just to our left, she's standing on all fours giving us the glare of a four hundred pound animal whose territory has been invaded by two creatures with neither fang nor claw for protection. She's close enough to feel her warm breath on our startled faces, imagine her white teeth on our soft necks. The next few seconds are years long.

The bear heaves herself up on her hind legs, shows off her formidable arsenal, drops back to all fours and begins to scramble down the boulders toward us.

I wave my hands over my head, yell out idiotically, "Bad Bear! Go away Now! Git," as though speaking to a large unruly dog.

From the corner of my eye, everything still in slow motion, I see Uncle bring the .30-06 around in an arch as the bear rears up again on her hind legs, now less than thirty feet from where we're shaking. I swing the Olympus up and snap off what will turn out to be four pictures. I have a mental image as clear as a summer dawn of my torn body found, these pictures telling the story of my death. Two of the shots will turn out to be blurred with the bear's rumbling forward movement, but the other two show every tensed muscle, every glistening drop of saliva in her open mouth.

She has a long jagged scar on the underside of her chest on the left side. That's what I remember the most vividly. That scar and thinking that the underside of a charging bear is not something I should be seeing. Even in that moment Uncle Walter keeps his head. He does not want to kill the bear. (He said afterward this was less about conservation and more about not wanting to pack the body of the creature all the way down the mountain once he'd shot her) He would, however, like to keep her from killing us. His shot is just wide and it does the trick. The bear turns her charge to our left and is swallowed by the woods a second later.

She is our Georgia balm, that bear. Uncle Walter and I are so pumped with adrenaline that we don't know whether to shake all over, fall down laughing or scream out a half dozen rebel yells into the woods. We do all three. Then we hug, cry that we love each other, swear we are just as sorry as we can be to hurt the other, and end sitting side by side retelling the story until the shaking stops and we figure to go on back to town and get some breakfast at Rebs.

On the way down the mountain, Uncle does his best to explain how frightened he is for me, marrying a man like that, is the way he puts it. He gets talking about all the change going on in Noisy Creek. The housing developments, the outsiders coming in and 'discovering' small town life.

"There's a new place, don't sell nothing but coffee. All kind a coffee. The Bean is the name. Folks in there payin' three, four dollars for a cup of coffee they could get over at Rebs for seventy-five cents. Course, used to be, cup a coffee was free if'n you had breakfast. Not no more. Ain't nothing the way it used to be."

"Some things are the same," I tell him.

"Not much and that there's the truth," he insists.

"I'm still your Red Crow. I still love you and want you to be as proud of me as I am of you."

He thinks about this. Clears his throat a time or two as we meander around a storm downed white hickory.

"Tell me 'bout that place down there. That Panama. They got deer?"

"Nope," I tell him and squeeze his hand. "No bear either."

Chapter Ten

I thought Uncle Walter and I had an exciting day. But this was before Uncles Earl and Neil made it back from their fishing expedition with what was left of Julio. We're all of us out at Green Acres sitting around a crackling log fire, swapping tales and catching up. Uncle Walter and I are embellishing The Lame Bear story, adding bits and pieces, some bits from memory some pieces pure lies. By this time that bear is twelve feet tall. Might have been a grizzly wandered down from up north. Teeth on the creature like razor sharp railroad ties. Claws like steel talons. That kind of thing.

The true part of the story, the part that creates the most unease in all of us, is the mystery of why that bear behaved the way it did. Black bear rarely threaten humans. Protection of cubs by a big ole mama being about the only reason a local bear would charge a person. Both Uncle Walter and I thought the pain and infection from that jagged shoulder wound might be contributing to the unnatural behavior. If Uncle had not fired the .30-06, both of us believe the animal would have attacked.

Preston is the one most concerned about the incident. He understands clearly that the folks buying his million dollar mountain retreats are not going to want quite that much wildlife roaming through their back yards. Dainty deer and strutting turkeys are good, hungry bears, not so much.

We narrowly avoid a fist fight when Preston suggests that Uncle Walter was negligent to have let that bear go.

"Allowed the escape of a hungry man-eating monster that is now running amuck amidst innocent home owners," is the way The Great Satin phrases it.

The man may not be from the south but he does have a way with words, no arguing that.

The unmistakable rattle and grind of Uncle Earl's truck pulling up in the front of the house thankfully ends this discussion before any bloodletting occurs.

I am already shaken from the bear encounter and have been growing increasingly worried as dusk turned to full dark with no sign of the fishing party. All three men were carrying cell phones. For two hours I have tried to calm my fears by inventing scenarios in which they could all be safe and yet not have seen fit to use those cell phones to call and let us know they were going to be late. The over consumption of alcohol was my first thought. But that was unlikely as I'd never known any of the three to drink enough to override their natural fear of Barr women folk. I finally settle on trouble with the boat motor while out of cell phone range as the most likely scenario while beating back images of bodies floating face down in murky water, hair streaming around their heads like so many broken promises.

So, when I hear the staccato rumble of Uncle Earl's beater, I am up and out the door well ahead of my aunts and uncles. The first thing I see when my eyes adjust to the night is Julio riding in the bed of the truck. I can just make out his dark head against the round corners of the rear window. When he stands to step off the open back of the truck, two things register at the same moment—his wide smile and his Dickie overalls. So relieved am I to see him that I am down the steps and into his arms before I notice the front of these overalls is encrusted with dried blood and what is unmistakably rancid fish innards.

"What have you done to my handsome, sophisticated man?" I wail at Uncle Earl while wiping hardened fish guts from the front of my sweatshirt and checking Julio for broken bones.

It turns out to be quite a story. Better even than The Lame Bear Tale, at least the way Uncle Earl tells it.

Three men and Beauregard, Uncle Earl's neurotic bulldog, in a fourteen-foot wooden skiff powered by a twenty-year-old Evanrude 80. Julio tells me later that with both Uncles tipping the scales at well over three hundred pounds and with Beauregard refusing to sit anywhere but on Uncle Earl's lap, it was a tight fit and a slow crawl across that lake in the early morning fog. As the sun threw its first pearly gray light over Martin's Ridge, they were motoring up an overgrown inlet at the back of the lake. One of those hidden estuaries that require the man in the squared off bow, in this case Julio, to kneel on the ribbed bottom and part the kudzu and skunk cabbage in order to thread the skiff through the eye of the cove.

As the greenery closed around the stern of the skiff, a great blue heron, startled from his stealthy pre-dawn frog gigging, gave a shattering squawk and flew directly over the bow of the boat. The way Uncle tells it, and by now he's well into his third Jax, there was some alarmed squawking and squealing inside the boat as well, in particular since the men had literally scared the shit out of the giant bird. There is some disagreement among the story tellers as to who it was that screamed like a little girl when the bird's call split the air, its awkward take off flight dragging its long gray legs inches above their heads, but they all agree it was Julio who received the largest portion of the goopy white substance dropped from less than a foot above them.

Once the laughter and the cussing and the rocking of the skiff died down, they claim to have moved deeper into the cove and, by true dawn, were casting their lines out onto the brackish water. Largemouth bass is what they were geared for. Light test line, lures that are the uncles own invention. Something they call Whirlibarrs. Lots of glittering rubber feelers and tiny reflective slats. It's the movement of the thing in the water that is the big secret between the two of them. I'm not sure Julio understands that letting him slide one of these lures onto a wrapped braid of his line is better than having his name penned into the family bible. But certainly, when this detail is revealed, I understand this gesture as the token of acceptance into the family that it most surely is.

Uncle Earl adjusts his ever-present Dickie Wedgie and shoots me a quick wink as he moves right along with the story.

Aunt Ruth always says that people will surprise you with their downright goodness if you just give them half a chance. Of course, this being Uncles Earl and Neil, that wasn't the end of the welcome into the family. I've been fishing with these two plenty of times. The way they do it is, the blue cooler starts the day filled with ice and aluminum cans of beer. As the day moves on, the beer cans get emptied and smashed flat (yes, that's right, usually on the broad foreheads of the uncles) and fish take the place of the beer on the ice. If they get lucky and catch a fish before they've made room for it in the cooler, well they just hang a line over the side and trail it in the water beside the skiff and drink a little faster.

Uncle Earl and Uncle Neil have both caught bass by the time the sun clears Martin's Ridge to the east of them. Uncle Earl has hauled in a six pounder and Uncle Neil has two smaller dinner-sized fish hung over his side of the boat. There is a fair amount of ribbing going on as Julio hasn't gotten so much as a nibble. Again, I happen to know that this is undoubtedly because there's a trick to using these Whirlibarrs of the Uncles. A certain periodic flick of the line is required to produce the correct movement of the lure through the murky water. It's the flashing motion that sends the bass leaping out of the water with the look of this irresistible spinner firmly embedded in his jaw.

I have no doubt that, within another hour or two, the uncles would have shared this family secret with Julio, but men being men, they enjoy rowdily pulling in fish while he sits wetting his line. Now is where the story goes off in three different directions.

"The next thing I know the boat is movin' sideways across the water. Your city boy here has the tip of the Johnson above his head and fish is tearin' off line like a sum . . . the line is whirring like a cicada summer. Ole

None of them will take the blame, but the general consensus is that with Uncle Neil already thrown off balance with the breaking of the starter rope, Julio thrashing to escape the snake, Beauregard leaping out of the boat for reasons only a neurotic bulldog would understand and Uncle Earl lunging for his dog, well, in all that confusion and movement, the skiff turns over dumping the whole mess of them, men, dog, snake, tackle and cooler into the brown waters of Blackjohn Lake.

As the waters close over his head, Julio can hear Uncle Earl yelling for him to save the beer. The moccasin, who is having a very bad day indeed, slides across Uncle Earl's chest, narrowly escaping momentary imprisonment in the depth of the billowing XXXXLarge overalls. When the splashing ends, Julio has horsed the bass into shore. Uncle Earl has saved the cooler, though to hear him tell it, the rescue came at great personal sacrifice which entitled him to exclusive rights to its contents. Uncle Neil lost his old metal tackle box but the rest of the gear floats long enough to be dragged to shore. Beauregard is clinging to the capsized boat and Uncle Earl swims back out and carries him ashore. This, we all assume, is the reason Uncle is covered with long red claw marks from the top of his head to the tips of his fingers.

Cell phones either sunk in the mud at the bottom of the lake or dripping water uselessly in the pockets of their owners, there is no help coming.

"What did y'all do?"

I'm still making completely unproductive swipes at the fish guts encrusted on Julio's overalls. Lord a-mighty, nothing smells just like year old fish innards.

"Why what could we do?" asks Uncle Neil. "We set right to emptying that there cooler."

Into the female head shaking this elicits, Uncle explains, "We hadda make room for the fish!"

Uncle Earl smashes his beer can against his forehead and goes right on with the story.

"Feelin' a good bit better after wettin' our whistles we just swim on out and wrestle the boat to shore."

Trying to decipher the story from the excited mix of three voices mostly talking at once, in two languages, the gist seems to be that using a rope thrown somewhat gingerly over the snakes recently vacated oak branch, they get the boat turned over. They remove the spark plugs, dry and replace them, but that old Evanrude isn't going to start without a complete overhaul. They aren't, however, up a lake without a paddle. It's broken off about half way up the handle, the blade itself has rotted through in the middle, but it moves the skiff through the water. Slowly and laboriously, and sitting very low in the water, but they're moving.

It's coming on full dark before another fisherman spots them on the far side of the lake and gives them a serious razzing and a tow. They load the skiff on the trailer in the dark and beat on the door of Jimmy John Foster's bait shop, boat rental, and official weigh station. Jimmy John is stretched out on his sofa in the little bitty apartment he keeps in the back of the shop, watching American Idol and about two beer short of a fine night's sleep when the Uncle's roust him.

It takes another hour to weigh Julio's bass. Well ok, it takes mere minutes to weigh the fish. It takes an hour to retell the story to Jimmy John and drink a congratulatory beer or three and snap off the requisite pictures of Julio with his lunker. That large mouth weighs fifteen pounds and two ounces. Three ounces shy of a state record. Twelve ounces over the previous Lake Blackjohn record. That none of them thinks to call home from the pay phone at the bait shop and that they all three strutt around in soggy clothes on a black night that is getting colder by the minute with no more sense than God gave a goose, well, with a catch that big, they can be forgiven.

When they finally leave Jimmy John and head home, a traumatized Beauregard refuses to be parted from Uncle Earl so is allowed to sit in the cab of the truck leaving insufficient room for all three men. The temperature now having dropped into the low 40's, the Uncle's take pity on Julio and give him a dry pair of overalls to wear so as not to have him ride in the open bed of the pickup in wet clothing. These are the same overalls, according to Uncle Earl, that he used to tie a gator to the side of the skiff two years ago. Evidently they have not been washed since that day of infamy.

It's quite a tale and they have the wet clothes, hair dried in tufts around their sun burned faces and, most importantly, the fish to back it up. More pictures are taken. The one of Julio in his stiff Dickies, his wavy hair still bearing the evidence of the Heron's aim, his lunker held by the gills, and the biggest smile ever on his gorgeous face, that one I'm planning to give to his Sainted Mother as a special gift from me to her. I'll buy a nice frame, maybe something in a pale gray wood to bring out the dried fish guts on the front of the overalls.

Chapter Ten

We don't make love. There's a moment in the shower when the possibility comes up, but wiley lunkers, bomb dropping birds, overturned boats and scarred bears have worn us both to a frazzle.

Spooning against Julio's warm back, the covers drawn up around our ears, I mumble, "This is nice. Just the sleeping together. No sex."

I think he's fallen asleep, am just dropping over the ledge into oblivion myself, when he rolls over, wraps me in his arms with my head resting on his chest and promises, "Mmm nice. We do again next year."

Next morning I am up before him, gulping my first cup of coffee, watching the sparrows discover the newly stocked bird feeder in the backyard. The air is so crisp I half expect the flutter of the birds wings to make it crackle, throw sparks of energy in an aura of expectancy. The bare limbs of the magnolias are starkly beautiful against the pale clear sky.

Coming awake after the first cup of caffeine, I sip the second cup and try to think my way through the maze of my future with Julio. It a difficult journey because the path blurs and weaves and moves on me from moment to moment. I have no hesitation about my love for him or his for me. My obstacle is fear of that very love. Each time I believe I've smoothed the road to happiness, I am overcome with a claustrophobic fear of abandonment. We may all adapt in the end but I'm afraid that Julio's beautiful golden skin and blue black hair have burned away my place in my Uncle Walter's heart forever.

Oh I can still turn back. I know how to construct a rope bridge or two to lead me home. I have been a southern redneck my whole life, I know the drill. I could walk away from Julio and my family would love and accept me, but I would be, always and forever, damaged goods. I understand, in a fuzzy sort of way, that when my parents died, I relied on the love of my aunts and uncles to save me from the dark. In a way, by loving Julio, I have rejected that familiar love.

Well maybe I haven't rejected the love, but I've turned my back on the values and unspoken rules of the society in which I was raised. That society may be changing rapidly, but, by bringing Julio home and declaring my love for a man whose heritage mark him as non-white, I've pretty much burned my bridge behind me. That I am absolutely certain that I am doing what is right for me, that I believe that Julio is the man who will make my life the most full and complete, that knowledge allows me to keep my grip on the swinging hemp, but it doesn't make the process any less frightening when I catch glimpses of the chasm below.

It's not just my bringing home a foreigner that has gotten folks around here upset. Once isolated Noisy Creek is in the grip of change. For over a hundred years there has been only sluggishly gradual movement in lifestyle and belief between generations. The grandchild's way of life barely different from the grandparents. True, in recent years more of us have gone off to college, and more and more of us have found it necessary to leave the area in order to find work. But we don't generally go far. Dothan, Americus, Columbus, maybe Atlanta for the really adventurous among us. Even I who, except for the soldiers and marines and sailors among what my aunts and uncles call the young folk, have gone the furthest from home and stayed away the longest, even I always meant to come home.

Now though, with these housing developments of Collins and Preston Yates, things are changing rapidly. Suddenly folks don't know everyone they see when they go to the Piggly Wiggly for a quart of buttermilk. At Rebs, local gossip shouted across tables laden with grits and eggs, sausage and biscuits, these tales are overheard by outsiders, folks who look up startled, screw up their faces in annoyance and blink their eyes at the back slapping and the ribbing and the just plain loudness of a normal morning restaurant breakfast in a town where pretty near everyone is family of one kind or another.

As I finish my second cup of coffee, the sky is a soft covering of dove gray, the sun no more than a glow over Hunley Mountain. When Julio joins me on the sun porch, we decide to have breakfast at Rebs. The old Rebs on this end of town, not the new fancier one that opened last year out near Leeville and Green Acres. Bundled up and walking under the bare late Fall trees, I am struck anew with the way memories layer every step I take here, every breath I draw.

I point out to Julio The Magnolia Tree Bakery. I promise him a sticky bun on the way back but I don't tell him that the summers of my junior and senior year I worked for Aunt Ruth at her spa The Baby Ruth Barr.

One of my jobs was to pick up the box of sticky cinnamon buns from The Magnolia Tree each morning on my way to work. Samuel was working that summer as stock boy for Longstreet pharmacy and we'd meet in the bakery and, while the buns were boxed, sip hot chocolates and make plans for the afternoon.

Now walking past the bakery, Julio's hand in mine, I feel again the weight of that heavy pink package, smell the warm cinnamon and sugar, see myself untying the white string, carefully removing each sticky roll and arranging it on Aunt Ruth's glass platter in preparation for the first customers to come through the doors at 8:00 ready for a day of pampering.

Cutting across Confederate Square, we lower our heads into a cold breeze and nearly bump into Collin. Julio and I are wearing borrowed jackets and stocking caps. I have my hood pulled up as well and my face half buried in Julio's shoulder. Collin is wearing jeans and a t-shirt.

"You two look like you're on an artic expedition."

Right now the warm breezes of Panama are calling me. I have forgotten how cold it can be on a sparkling Fall morning in Georgia. Stopping to talk, I lift first one foot then the other, pace in place in an attempt to keep warm. Collin and Julio are making plans to see the Hunley Mountain development. I'm fantasizing about hot coffee in thick white mugs, a warm plate of eggs, grits and sausage, all enjoyed in one of Rebs red leatherette booths.

I didn't sleep well last night, kept waking with that bear looming over me, her toothy mouth dripping bloody saliva, her intentions obvious. Just before I got up, the dream had morphed so that I was unable to lift my arm to protect myself, my hand weighted to my side by a heavy rock I was unable to drop. Now I stuff my hand deep in the pockets of Aunt Snickers jacket, rub my thumb along the edge of my engagement ring. Stop the instant I realize what I'm doing.

The heat stuns me as we step inside Rebs. Nicely stunned. Gloriously stunned.

"Goo Goo!" call out two Barr cousins, a Martin auntie, four Ragsdale boys and the Burnett twins.

"Y'all look frozen near 'bout half to death."

"How's your Uncle Walter an them?"

"Get yoself over here right this instant and g'me some sugar." This from Auntie Sally.

The Ragsdale boys are sitting in the far back booth, the one next to the space heater. They get up as we make our rounds, indicate with a sweep of a hand that, the southern gentlemen their mama raised them to be, they are giving up their table to us temperature challenged folk.

"Y'all set here by the heater. Where you can warm that thin blood."

If there is an undercurrent of disapproval, a slight hesitation in this welcome, it is so subtle that only a local would see its shadow in the exchanged glances, the eyes cast downward. A part of the dynamic here is that, as a Barr, I am a member of the ruling class in this here town. There is something in all of us that delights in the mighty dropping down a peg or two. The fact that I refuse to acknowledge this downgrade in my status is a confusion and disappointment to my friends and kin alike. We're all of us adjusting here, feeling our way through the fog of change.

Mary Ann wipes down the gray Formica table and sets two heavy mugs on paper placemats decorated with drawings of our local statuary. The Confederate Soldier, General Lee, Jeff Davis, Traveller with the General sitting proud on his capable back, all are intertwined with kudzu and Muscatine, Magnolia and Pecan trees. Before we settle into the warm booth everyone in the restaurant must see the ring.

Two fiery carats square cut and set flat in a wide gold band. It's beautiful. I love it. I do. It's just sort of heavy on my hand is all. And maybe all these folks need to back off a pace or two. I'm feeling just a teensy bit peckish. I truly think I might be coming down with something.

Most everyone has met Julio out at Travellers Park. He shakes hands with the men, kisses the wrists of the blushing women. Watching him I think how different he looks. He fits in better here in Noisy Creek in these borrowed, store-bought duds. Of course he's still wearing his own tailored chinos and soft cotton shirt, but Collin's Carhartt jacket and stocking hat are a nice outer disguise.

"What you gonna do for the talent contest Saturday?" the Burnett twins ask.

I've been trying to forget that I agreed to be a contestant in this Redneck Goddess Contest. The twins, Gloria and Gladys, have been given permission to display their talent together. They're doing some kind of dancing, juggling routine that involves full cans of beer and a fireman's pole. From the look on the faces of the Ragsdale boys I predict this display of redneck ability is going to be a big hit with the male judges. Aunt Snickers has suggested that I give a power point lecture on the local moths and butterflies. Show some slides and knock their socks off with a few interesting bug facts is the way Auntie put it to me. Somehow I do not see this competing successfully with pole dancing and beer juggling.

"What did y'all draw in the contest hunting and fishing lottery?" Gladys asks.

Evidently the twins will be fishing for catfish on something Preston Yates has labeled section twelve of Lake Blackjohn. The girls are thrilled as there isn't much a good ole boy judge likes better than fried catfish. Since the contestants will all be cooking whatever they've managed to shoot, hook or track down, this is good news indeed—fried catfish trumps near about anything else in the grinds department. Dear God how much must I love my Aunt Snickers to have agreed to be involved in this mess? Though, come to think of it, my compliance had more to do with that second Schiltz I shared with Uncles Earl and Neil than with love of family.

When I admit that I don't know yet where or what I'll be doing in the hunting/fishing competition, the twins get on their little pink rhinestone encased cell phones and quickly inform me that, since I am the only contestant who hasn't yet come by the Yatesville office, by elimination I will be hunting deer on the backside of Martin's Ridge.

That settled, Gloria and Gladys are frantic to know what I'll be wearing in the beauty portion of the contest. They're secretive about their own outfits but hint of cut off jeans that show more butt and jewels than denim. When I tell them plain jeans and a cotton t-shirt are my choice, the silent shock they enter into is an excuse to end the conversation and make our way to our lovely table so close to the space heater that, within five minutes, I can feel my toes wiggling in my tennis shoes again.

Julio spends a long time with the plastic menu before I recommend the eggs and sausage.

"This will come with the greets?"

"I'll ask Mary Ann to substitute something else if you don't want grits."

"Fruit?"

"Not hardly."

I order us both Rebs breakfast special with sausage, spicy hot for me, mild for Julio. The order confuses Mary Ann who can't understand why Julio doesn't want his food extra spicy.

"They don't do that in Panama," I tell her. "You're thinking of Mexico."

Still confused she brings a side of jalapenos specially for him, sits it beside his plate with an accommodating smile.

I'm just mopping up the last of my grits with egg yolk when Samuel walks in. I wave him over and scoot around to the other side of the booth beside Julio while Samuel perches opposite us.

"Heard you got engaged," he mumbles reaching his hand across the table to shake with Julio. "Nice rock," he says eyeing the ring, but he won't meet my eye.

Maybe my attraction to him out at Traveller's Park was just the shock of seeing him after so long, had more to do with wanting the comforts of home than with the man himself. This morning, I can see that he is a very attractive redneck, just my old type and someone who would keep me in the good graces of my Uncle Walter, but I'm happy to be sitting beside Julio. The little tremor deep inside when anyone mentions the ring or marriage, that's just my way of showing how thrilled I am. It's a tremor of joy, not a symptom of the gaping black hole trying to open at my feet.

"Hope she wears that one longer than the one I gave her," Samuel mumbles.

I had forgotten that the two of us were engaged. For about two hours. Our junior year up in Athens. Samuel had given me his grandma's ring, we spent an hour making plans for the future and another hour with me crying and trying to catch my breath and explaining to him that the ring was too tight. It didn't fit. It was cutting off the circulation to my hand. Here look, is my whole hand turning black? I need to move. I can't breathe. That kind of deal.

I reach across the table and lay my hand over Samuels.

"We were really young Samuel." My only excuse for breaking his heart and then forgetting I'd even done so.

"You more than me," he says and this time he does look into my eyes.

"You hear the new statue came in?" he changes the subject. "The one of Bessie Smith for out there at the Martins Ridge Park."

It pleases me to think of how the name of the park itself is going to be another way to divide locals and invaders. The park and the housing development may eventually be accepted into the community, but locals are always going to call the area Martins Ridge no matter how many signs and statues name it Yatesville.

"I thought it wasn't going to be unveiled until just before they announce the winner of this silly beauty contest."

"Uh huh, not even your Aunt Snickers has seen it. But it's here and somebody had to get it off loaded. Me and Davey Burnett helped build the gazebo deal it's gonna set under so that little twi . . . that gal Kristen paid us to set it up. Made us sign a contract not to reveal anything about the statue. Like we were in on a state secret or some such and our word wasn't promise enough to keep quiet."

"So, what's it look like?"

Samuel's grin tells me we are in for real treat when Kristen Yate's creation is unveiled the last day of the Redneck Beauty Contest.

"Let's just say you've seen something right similar to it before."

"So it's not original?" I ask.

Samuel laughs and grins at me, "Oh it's original all right. That it is."

"Who is this Bessie Smith?" Julio asks and I realize that we've been excluding him from the conversation. Something he is careful never to do when I am with his friends in his country. Samuel and I tell him the story together in the way of children who grew up together. It takes a while. I'm on my fifth cup of coffee by the time we finish. So many things I take for granted, Julio does not know. It's the same in Panama for me. With no sense of the history of the place, everything must be explained to me and still I miss nearly all the nuance.

Samuel and I must first explain about the War of Northern Aggression before we can begin to talk about Sherman's march through our great state. Along the way Samuel refers to Lincoln as The Great Manipulator which leads us into a half hour diversion because Julio's limited

American history has taught him to see this war mongering president as a hero.

"You want a hero?" Samuel asks, "let me tell you about General Lee."

For a half hour we take Julio through the loops and turns of General Lee and our boys in gray as they fight heroically to save the homeland from the invading northern army. Finally we get to the legend of Bessie Smith. We tell about how a scouting party of Yankees came through Noisy Creek. A battered company of Sherman's boys lost from up near the Chattahogee.

"Hell," Samuel laughs. "Only Yankees could lose themselves while following a river.

"These Yankees," Julio asks, "they are Americans, no? The same as you?"

"NOOO!" Samuel and I both shout him down.

"I do not understand. This war that was so long ago, it was to free the black people, yes?"

"NOOOOO! It was to enslave the rural southland to the urban north. Freeing the slaves was just a handy excuse for the invasion."

On and on we go, through the maze of long ago battles in congress and the admittance of free vs. slave states and the plantation system vs. factories. Eventually we settle on the explanation that while slavery was a horrible institution, of that there is no doubt, it was not the overriding reason for the War Between the States. By this time Julio's eyes are glazing over, and the entire restaurant has gotten into the discussion.

To me Julio whispers, "This war it ended many years past, yes?"

Not really.

Finally we get to Bessie Smith. It's Auntie Sally, now sitting on the leatherette bench beside Julio who pats his knee and tells the story.

"Them Yankee boys they was lost is what they were. They come staggering into town on a day when the old men and boys was out huntin'. Was hard times then. The men was all gone. Little bitty boys no mo' than ten had done run off, joined the battle. Was just women and chil'un and men too old to ride. Was the women was runnin' things."

"Bessie Smith, you met her kin," Aunt Sally says to Julio, "out at that get together at the park the other day. They is no more Smiths here about. Bessie, she only had the one daughter, the Smith men was all killed off or wounded so bad they none of 'em married. But the daughter, what was her name now?   LeeAnne that was it. Anyways, LeeAnne she married one a the Barr boys is what she done."

Here there is a confusion of voices all claiming that Auntie is mistaken and that LeeAnne Smith, daughter of Bessie, had in fact married into their own families. While this heated discussion is whirling through the restaurant a couple in a Lexus pulls into the gravel parking lot, comes as far as the open front door before backing their designer jeans out again. I whisper to Julio that I'll explain about all this confusion later. I also run my foot up his leg under the table to remind him that he promised it would be a whole year before we had another night without sex.

"Well," Aunt Sally reclaims the floor, "if'n y'all are done with yo interruptin' of an ole lady, I will just go on with this here tale."

In the south, I don't care how silly, crazy, loud or wrong an older person may be, that person is always treated with respect. They're sort of like the rattle trap busses in Panama called Red Devils. No matter what, they have the right of way.

"So, as I was sayin', these here Yankee boys come wanderin' into town wantin' food and anything else they might discover if you understand my meanin'. Bessie Smith, she seen 'em first and she sent little Janie Goodin with instructions for the other womens. See Bessie she was old, too old to be putting any ideas in the heads a these marauders. That's what she was hopin'."

"Whilst Bessie was talking with them Yankees, sort a slowin' 'em down some, the other womens they was makin' a welcome for those boys. Only had one long rifle between 'em. The old men had the other un out huntin' for game. Now this I know for a certainty, ain't no disputin' this here," Auntie pauses long enough for the rest of us to nod our heads in agreement. No way would any of us give her an argument. Didn't matter what she said. That look there, that hard stare could send any and all of us into the hell of an elder displeased.

"T'was a Foster gal was up in the steeple a the Babtist church yonder with that rifle trained on them northern boys."

"That there is the way I always have heard it told," we all agree, "Yes ma'am, ain't no disputin' that. Was a Foster gal."

Her credibility restored Auntie goes on with the tale. "The rest a the women folk they was preparin' a respite for them Yankees. Yes they was. Sweet tea and biscuits is what I heard was brung out to be shared."

When no one objects to this rendition, Auntie goes on. She tells Julio directly, "Wasn't much to share back then. Was hard times. I mean hard times." We all nod our heads just as if any of us has ever missed a meal in our lives. "Them Yankees was mighty hungry themselves being separated from they own army. Lost is what they was. Did I already say that?"

"Yes Ma'am you did, but it's a fact worth sharing again."

"So anyways, them boys was happy to get them special made hard tack biscuits and tea. See the thing is, their arrival had been anticipated by ole Bessie and the women folks of this here town. Sherman's boys was known for burning and stealing and raping. There, I said it right out loud. That's what they was doin' y'all. Was raping the land and the womens. Was destroying the southland as deep as they could. Tryin' to force us to give up the cause is what."

This is the moment when I half expect someone, one of the Ragsdale boys would be my best guess, to unfurl the bonnie blue flag. We all of us sit up straighter, nod our heads, promise each other with our eyes to never give up the cause. I mean never. Not that between us we could give you a precise definition of what the cause is exactly. But that matters not at all. It's in our blood this southern pride. We might be better at knowing what it ain't than what it is, but we will still to this day fight to the death to defend it. It is not lost on me that the man sitting beside me, the man whose ring I am wearing on my confederate finger, is an affront to this here cause, a blatant example that the cause may indeed be lost. I am telling you straight out, these are confusing times in the southland.

"So what I'm telling y'all is that those vittles had been waitin' for them boys for a good long time before that rag tag bunch wandered into town. Well, them Yankees done gobbled up ever last crumb and was just a startin' to cast their eyes around town. See what there was worth stealin' or claimin', if ya catch my drift. Ceptin' within just a very few minutes them boys had discovered that southern cookin' didn't agree with 'em. Not a t'all."

Julio has picked up his spoon and is absently poking around in his untouched grits.

"Rat poison is what I understand. Maybe coulda been lye. Whatever it was," Auntie goes on, "by the time the old men came back from the hunt just before dark what they found is a mess a dead Yankees litterin' up Confederate Square out yonder. Now, here is where the story gets a bit muddled. See some folks say them boys was buried out there where the welcome sign is as ya come into Noisy Creek. They may be correct. Ya ever notice how the grass is extra bright green and grows sort a high and wild rat there in front a that sign?"

We all allow as how we have noticed that phenomena, yes we have.

"Other folk now, they'll tell ya that them Yankees is buried out there in Leeville where that Green Acres deal is now. Could be either one. Could be both. Might be neither. To my way a thinkin' we got us plenty a places round here to bury dead Yankees."

This seems an appropriate sentiment on which to make our exit. As Julio and I walk back to Aunt Ruths I try to explain to him that none of what he just heard is exactly historical. In fact, it's all a big fat lie made up by Crazy Colonel Connery to bring in tourists, those damn fool re-enactors of The War Between the States. Given the towns love of the story and bickering over the details it soon becomes apparent that trying to deny the tale, trying to explain to Julio why an entire town would make something like this up is more difficult than just going along with the story. Which is what I do. By the time we're walking in the door of the house on Clayton Lane, I've given up the need for honesty and am conceding that indeed, there really must have been a Bessie Smith. My only concern is that Julio seems less focused on the southern heroics of the tale than on the dead Yankees buried somewhere in the red dirt of Noisy Creek.

Chapter Eleven

When I stepped out of the Tocumen Airport into the steamy air of Panama City two years ago, my high school Spanish coupled with one of those computer 'Speak Spanish like a native' CDs with the cross word puzzles and mechanical voice modulator, enabled me to communicate like a mentally challenged three year old. When I began seeing Julio, my Spanish language skills took a large step up. Turns out a horizontal position is actually a much faster as well as more enjoyable, way to learn a language. Funny they don't have beds instead of desks in foreign language classes across the world. I admit my first proficiency was in body parts, but the progression moved quickly on to a more general expertise and I now can say with confidence that I speak the language like an intelligent three year old.

So, when I answer the living room phone to find The Sainted Mother on the other end of the line, it's Spanish I am trying to speak with her. The woman speaks English. Better than Julio actually because she wined and dined and hobnobbed for forty years with the Americans who were running the canal before Jimmy Carter turned management over to her own country. Still, out of respect, I talk to her in Spanish, and thus feel like a verbally challenged child. She is not happy to have gotten me on the phone instead of The Young Prince, but, since he isn't here at the moment and it is looking like, over all her objections, I may end up as her daughter-in-law, she is stiffly polite.

"I understand you have agreed to marry my son," she accuses me in her language.

"Yes, Senora Monterey. He asked me to marry him and I have said yes."

"So I understand," she says flatly.

Well, not exactly an exuberant welcome to the family, but she is speaking with me. A first. In the past she has managed to talk to me through Julio or one of her daughters. *Tell your friend not to sit in that chair. I'm sure she doesn't recognize it as such, but it is an antique. Ask your brother's friend if she would like to borrow more suitable clothes to wear to dinner. And once-point out to your brother that where she comes from they don't know any better than to eat their salad with their dinner fork, but in this house we are ladies and gentlemen.*

In the beginning Julio simply ignored his mother's rudeness to me. Then he began to reprimand her gently, the loving son making a request. Finally, and this was The Wrong Fork Incident, he stood up from her well set mahogany table lifting me from my chair beside him, kissed my cheek and addressed his mother in such rapid fire Spanish that the only word of the entire tirade I understood was 'amor' which was the only word I needed to hear. We have not been back to her home nor have I spoken with her until today when I hear her tight voice on the other end of the phone line.

So when she gives me slow and careful instructions as to what time her flight will be coming into Atlanta and ends the conversation by ordering me to have her son call her so that she is ensured that a competent person will actually be meeting her plane, this is progress in our relationship. She still hates me but I am now worthy of her direct scorn.

Julio is exploring the town on his own. Without his panicky fiancée. He and I aren't fighting exactly, but a short time apart seemed this morning like a Jim Dandy idea. I had a moment or two which might possibly have stretched into an entire morning of bitchiness, when Julio began talking of children. How many, what schools they would attend, the sort of talk that is I understand common among the newly engaged. It isn't that I don't want children or that I'm not looking forward to beautiful babies who are a lovely blend of Julio and me. But the man insisted on talking about the subject when I was trying to put together the stupid power point presentation for the idiotic Redneck Beauty Contest in which I allowed myself to be roped into participating. It was the idea of that contest that set me off. What else could it have been? At any rate, Julio kissed me on the top of my red head and walked out the door leaving me alone with my panic.

When he returns to the house in the early afternoon, as my way of apologizing for my earlier insanity, we take Uncle Earl's truck out to that flat patch of rural route 6 and I teach Julio to drive a stick shift. He picks it up pretty fast considering that Uncle Earl's truck has no third gear whatsoever, the clutch is maybe a half inch from the floor and the brake has to be pumped half a dozen times before the vehicle begins its slow screeching stop. When I'm sure he can handle it without driving us off the mountain, we come back toward town and hang a left up the backside of Martins Ridge.

The old make out spot is empty, so he backs onto the lookout point and we climb into the bed of the truck to enjoy the view. Snuggled down with our backs resting against the cab we're looking out over a wide valley of dull greens and browns under a steel gray sky with an occasional autumn maple glowing gemlike in all that blandness. I wonder how this scene looks to Julio coming as he does from a country of more vibrant greens. Before I can ask him this, he reveals an agenda of his own.

"You have been engaged to Samuel?"

"For about two hours. I was young. Not ready to be married. I panicked. I gave back the ring and that was sort of the beginning of the end of the relationship."

A striped chipmunk makes his way along the branch of a pine tree, his cheeks bulging with the last of the pine nuts to be stored for the winter.

"You are doing some of this panic now also I think. We are doing, you and I, a little dance, yes? Close for a moment, then you push back, then more close again."

"We are yes. Nice way to put it. But every time we come together we are closer and the spaces when I hold you away are shorter. Don't you think?"

I twist around wanting to see his face. I know I have trouble committing. This isn't the first time I've tried to saddle this particular horse. I've never been in therapy but I have an achingly clear understanding that losing both my parents as a child has left me reluctant to count on people. In bad moments, when I become again a frightened nine year old, I fear my love has some sort of peculiar power to kill. So that using a weird childlike logic, I'm really saving people when I refuse to commit to loving them. What turns

me from going down this road is that even as a child I
understood that, while my parents may have abandoned
me for death, dozens of other people who loved me did not
die off on me but stayed right beside me, were there for me
whenever I needed them. That these are the very folks I
have now antagonized with my love of a beautiful dark man
is simply adding another dimension to my challenge.

Julio knows all this about me. We've been going
together for over a year. We have spent most of our time
getting to know each other from a prone position, but we
have talked during the rest periods. I know all about his
family's political ambitions for him, his desire for another
way of life. He knows most everything about my
insecurities as well as my need for independence. Here in
Noisy Creek he's seeing for himself where I come from. At
the same time, for the first time, we are together almost
every day. I am mostly enjoying this new intimacy. I am.
But it is also chafing some on my need for solitude, scraping
a bit on my fears.

The chipmunk has finally noticed us. He is up on his
hind legs, still in the pine tree but now on the lowest
branch. He pumps his tail a time or two, wobbles his
whiskers. Finally he seems to decide we are no threat and
he drops back down, gives us one more cover girl,
over-the-shoulder look and scampers up the tree
disappearing into the higher branches.

"I am asking you," Julio says in a voice so soft I almost
miss the question, "if you are certain you want to marry
me."

I flip around instantly, kneel in the hard bed of the
truck, need us to be face to face. For an instant I see my

life without this man. Noisy Creek. A local boy. Maybe
Samuel, maybe someone like Samuel in a hundred
different ways. I see a warm flowing life of ease
surrounded by my family. Weekend get togethers. Trips
to Atlanta. Long summer weekends on the gulf shore.
Children whose skin is pale and whose hair is the usual
Barr red. It would all be so easy. Except that I have fallen
in love with Julio and with the life he and I will create
together. Trying to imagine a life without him closes my
throat tight, turns my future gray and lifeless.

"I am absolutely positively certain," I tell him in
Spanish, "and yes I am scared about half to death."

"Yes. I am afraid but I want us to spend our lives
together," I say in English.

"You ain't getting rid a me," I promise in
redneck-ese and with my best washed-in-the-blood
prayer, I beg the good Lord to soothe the frightened child
and make all these declarations turn out to be true.

Julio pulls me down onto the bed of the truck,
unzips our jackets so that I feel the heat of his body as we
stretch full length wrapped together as close as we can get
through three layers of clothing.

"How about you," I whisper between kisses, "are you
sure you want to marry me after seeing me in all my
hillbilly glory?"

His answer is deep and warm and wet.

Julio and I spend the next week sketching out a
picture of our future. As each day and night passes, the
outlines grow more clear. As we fill in and flesh out the
picture using the colors of hope and desire, my fear grows

dimmer. The insecurity is still there. Under all the plans and hopes, there's still a lost little girl clutching her knees and shaking, but most days the image is only a ghostlike reminder of someone else's past.

We talk about buying one of the homes Collin is building up on Hunley Mountain but Aunt Ruth insists that we stay in her house in town when we are in Noisy Creek and we decide that, for the moment at least, this is the better idea. My relatives are still, if not enthusiastic, then at least willing to forego the tar and feathers and I'm still worried about The Sainted Mother. Julio is insistent that she is all bark and no bite. Yeah, but her bark is really loud and I find it extremely annoying.

Uncle Walter and I have reached an uneasy truce, my plans with Julio an impregnable wall of disapproval between us. Still, our love tunnels under the wall, pops up incorrigibly in smiles and touches and remembrance of shared history and need. Some days I can't imagine ever feeling free and easy in his company again and others I think Aunt Ruth is correct and love will, eventually, break down the wall.

The morning light shines through the chalk dust in my nephew Jake's fourth grade class. Jake informed me that he would rather I had brought him a monkey, but he supposed Julio and I would do as his show and tell. I set up my laptop and we show a few slides of moths and butterflies but the slides the kids really like are the ones of the canal and of Panama City. I tell what I know about the country's flora and fauna and I let Julio field the rest of the questions. He weaves the story of the French attempt to cut a ditch through the isthmus, followed by the American accomplishment and his own countries management now that Georgia's own Jimmy Carter brokered a deal with President Torrijas to turn the canal over to the Panamanians. This story requires the use of a world map. Many of the kids seem to think Panama is a part of Mexico. One little girl is quite certain the world consists of America with Canada a thin strip at the top side and Mexico a dark blur along the bottom and that's it.

"All the rest is ocean," she explains and then seeing the look on the face of her teacher she adds, "and maybe some islands."

Mrs. Clark promises to begin a review of geography the very minute we finish our little show.

I love watching Julio with the kids, his forthright easy way with them. Hardly anything is more annoying than an adult talking down to a child.

To the little girl who thinks the world is a bit smaller than reality he says, "You are the center of all the world. The older you get, the more you read the books and listen with your teachers, the bigger the world will be."

I hold the gorgeous man's hand as we leave the elementary school. I'm wondering what our children will look like.

The Decompression Room of The Baby Ruth Barr is as elegant and comfortable as I remember it. Decorated in soft apricots and creams with high ceilings and windows along the roof line, this is where Aunt Ruth's customers come to relax after their spa treatments or exercising at the gym or where they just drop by for a little relaxation and gossip before going home to mop floors and can green beans. Today it is where the whole bunch of us Redneck Goddess contestants are having our mandatory meeting. Aunt Snickers is in charge. Which means we are all of us sitting up straight and I am limiting myself to only the occasional snotty look in the direction of Lizzie Ragsdale.

When Lizzie pranced into the room five minutes ago in her usual outfit of jeans cut low enough to show off her Brazilian wax and some toddlers t-shirt stretched across her braless tits, I leaned over to the Burnett twins and commented, "Redneck slut is more like it."

Unfortunately, as I may have already mentioned, the Barr Aunties have excellent, one might even say supernatural, hearing. My comment, while perfectly true, earned us all a five minute lecture on what did and did not constitute ladylike behavior and what would and would not be tolerated during the course of this contest. At the end of this Miss Southern Manners lecture we were required to parrot, "Yes Miss Barr," just as though we meant it. Aunt Ruth who was also in attendance felt the need to walk across the room and take a seat next to me on the sofa where she took my hand in hers, all the better to squeeze the life out of me if I misbehaved again.

The contest is to take place over three days. Friday morning will be the beauty and talent contest. I'm not sure what the aunties had in mind when they came up with the idea of dressing in denim but evidently they've gotten wind of some of the planned costumes because there are now restrictions on butt cheek exposing short shorts, thong bikinis and nipple pasties.

When these additional rules are announced Lizzie Ragsdale earns herself an auntie warning stare by whining, "Talk about taking all the fun out of a thing!"

The talent displays must now to be approved by the aunties before we get up on stage and present our gifts to the world at large. A clip board and sheet are right now being passed around the room and we are all to explain just what we will be doing for this portion of the contest.

This announcement causes the Burnett twins to exchange worried glances and Lizzie to complain, "It's right hard to explain in writin'."

I yearn to tell the little twit to call it what the boys on the football bus always did. A Lizzie Special. But I already cannot feel three fingers on the hand clutched in Aunt Ruth's, so I keep my big mouth shut even though it's damn near killing me to do so.

Friday afternoon will be the 4x4 contest. Four beater four-wheel-drive vehicles, assigned by draw; all of them with some minor mechanical problem. We will be required to repair the vehicle and then barrel around a course which is already marked off on the south side of Martin's Ridge and which we are welcome to preview. I've already seen the course. Pretty near everybody in the room has done the same. It's mostly mud and a narrow creek crossing. Nothing dangerous or challenging to young women who learned to drive on their daddy's tractors. There are sixteen contestants and four vehicles so the luck of the draw is going to determine who climbs into a pristine four wheeler and who ends up with very sloppy fourths. We'll each have one hour to fix the vehicle and run the course. That will give the reverse mechanics thirty minutes to break things again before the next four contestants begin the race.

Saturday will be the hunting/fishing contest. We all know where we've been assigned. We're expected to bring our own gear. I'll be on the north side of Martin's Ridge and will be packing my Winchester .30-06. The rules say we are to kill, clean and carry the game back to the starting point at the Yatesville park. The next afternoon, Sunday, we will be serving whatever we killed the day before to the judges and to those folks who come to see the contest. Which will be every living soul in Noisy Creek. It goes, according to Aunt Snickers, without saying that we will all be in the church of our choice on Sunday morning before the final afternoon of the contest.

None of this information is news to any of us wanna be Redneck Goddesses. Even I, who have entered only as a favor to my Aunt Snicker and have no real interest in being crowned Queen of Noisy Creek, even I have not avoided the heavy, darn near electrical, mist of excited gossip in which the town is blanketed. Now though, Aunt Snickers introduces Preston Yates with a promise that he has a surprise for all of us. As he walks to the front of the room, Preston is puffed up like the only rooster in the henhouse.

He explains to us in his deep baritone radio announcer voice that the contest will be taped by a real Hollywood movie maker. The word Hollywood is spoken the way I imagine an orthodox Jew might utter his secret name of his Lord Yahweh. With a wide sweep of his arm,

Preston ushers into the salon a young women in a red wool pants suit toting a camera almost as big as herself. Cassandra Gallant will be documenting the contest. All of us will be receiving a copy of the finished product. Ms. Gallant reminds me of a nervous Cardinal lighting for the first time on a new backyard bird feeder.

The room fills with an excited buzz even before Preston has finished speaking. Two of us stand instantly, one of us is rubbing her hand to bring back the circulation.

"I have been called a good many things," Lizzie shouts, "but naive ain't never been one a 'em."

Amen to that, I think, and I choose my words carefully. I know enough to talk to this Yankee like the college educated young woman I am. Big words and a firm voice, that's what this carpetbagger will understand.

"Mr. Yates," I begin as Lizzie and I walk across the salon to stand in the front of the room with Preston and the now twittering Cassandra Gallant. "I will not be a part of a project that allows some slick Hollywood producer to slice and edit and make me and the rest of the town I love into a parody and a laughing stock. What exactly do you plan to do with this little movie project?"

Preston looks surprised by our objections, I might even say nervous. Aunt Snickers appears vindicated. She smiles sweetly at her beau and indicates with a ladylike shrug that this was his big idea, he can explain it.

"Well now," he begins with a thorough clearing of his throat, "as I have already said, all of you will be getting a free copy of this quite costly project as a keepsake of your involvement."

Lizzie and I stare at him. Sometimes it's better to just shut up and let 'em sweat.

Eventually he clears his throat enough to cough up the truth. "Parts of the documentary will be included in a sales video for Yatesville estates."

"Wait now!" Ellie Clark nearly yelps, "how do I know y'all are gonna show the shots a me looking my best and not some ole picture after that there 4x4 deal? All covered in mud and whatnot."

"Hell yeah!," chime in the Burnett twins, "and once y'all have got them pictures they could end up any ole where. On the internet. Anywheres."

The film maker herself now joins the fray.

"I am in fact hoping to market a slightly differently edited version of the documentary," Cassandra explains. "I will be shooting all of the contest. The pretty and the messy. That's the appeal of this contest. The reason I'm here filming. Hoping to make you all famous."

"Infamous is more like it," I mutter and Lizzie, bless her slutty heart, backs me up with an amen. It looks to me like the room is about evenly divided between those whose southern instincts are blaring a warning against outsiders and those who really, really want to be movie stars.

"Here's the thing," I say to my cousins. "Y'all know that Lizzie and I have had our differences. Every one of you has heard each of us say something about the other one that doesn't bear repeating. We're family, Lizzie and me. We're allowed to poke fun, point out our worst features and, on occasion, be downright rude and obnoxious with one another."

"I don't see what..." Preston Yates begins but a look from Aunt Snickers shuts his mouth.

"But," I go on, "if an outsider comes in here and I overhear him say one single even slightly tainted word against my beloved cousin Lizzie, well you know for a fact the fur is gonna fly. Well, this movie seems to me pretty much the same deal. It's one thing for Noisy Creek to laugh at ourselves with this contest, to use it to demonstrate pride in who we are. It's something else entirely for it to be twisted around by outsiders so that we look like ignorance hillbillies."

It takes almost two hours of yelling and offers to have attorneys negotiate contracts and promises to walk out of the contest and counteroffers, but we finally compromise by agreeing that the documentary can be made but that each and every one of us must approve of the finished product. In the end I feel as if I've just been tricked out of my birthright, Preston announces sadly that he is, 'deeply disappointed' and Aunt Snickers assures us that she 'could not be prouder of y'all.' If a good negotiation is one in which nobody is happy with the outcome, well than, we have struck a right fine deal.

There is some whispered discussion between Preston Yates and Aunt Snickers about previously assumed return on investments, but in the end Mr. Yates, more or less graciously, announces the prizes. Third runner up will receive a $1,000 savings bond. Second runner up will be awarded a $2,000 bond. The winner will receive a new Jeep Wrangler in her choice of color and the honor of unveiling the statue of local hero Bessie Smith at the culmination of the contest.

Lizzie and I go to lunch at Rebs. It seems like as good a time as any to bury the hatchet. That and she has some gossip to share about cousin Wanda Clark, head cheerleader and uncontested prom queen three years running.

"An ass the width of an ax handle, I swear. Two hundred pounds if she's an ounce and ya know that fancy pants lawyer husband a hers is running around with . . .."

Chapter Twelve ★

The old house needs a coat of paint but the roof is new and the place still sits firm and solid on its foundations. The great grandson of General Lee meets us at the front porch steps, his tail stirring the air every bit as fast as his ancestors did the day we rousted a baby badger. We're taking Uncle Walter over to Goggins barbeque for supper, but have stopped off here first because I want Julio to see the house in which I was raised. I am unexpectedly nervous now that we're here. Keep pulling at the dogs ears, rubbing his speckled belly, talking nonsense to the animal to distract myself from this sudden anxiety.

When the front door screen slams I look up from where I'm squatting beside the dog to see Uncle Walter in his best shirt, the green one that matches his eyes, the one I helped him choose at the Sears store over in Dothan when he was courting Susan Sinclair all those years ago. Seeing him there, his face a funny mix of pride and nervousness brings those days right back into the moment.

"Whatever happened to Susan?" I ask him.

Julio looks as though he will never be able to follow a conversation around here if he lives to be a hundred. Uncle grins and I can see him relax around the edges of his mouth.

"She up and married that Jones boy from Americus. They got four younguns last I heared."

Uncle's hair is stiff with Vitalis, his Wranglers brand new. His boots gleam with a spit polish like he used to warn me about when I was a young dress wearing girl hanging around with clever country boys. Seeing him like this, all duded up in preparation for going to dinner with me and a man of whom he does not approve and yet is doing his best to make peace with, it brings fat salty tears to my eyes. I hug his neck. When I pull away and both men see my wet cheeks, the two of them exchange a look of befuddlement that makes me cry harder.

"She's always been a hard one to figure," Uncle tells Julio, but he keeps right on rubbing my back. Winks at me as we go inside.

It's been almost five years since I last stepped foot on this green and beige mottled linoleum. The smell of Joy dish detergent and Pine Sol mixes with the musk of old wood and the six slices of bacon Uncle prepares for breakfast every day of the year. The white Westinghouse range still has a chip like a black thumbprint at the rounded corner closest to the porcelain sink. I was four when Daddy bought Mama that range to replace the wood stove she'd been cooking on since she moved into the house as his new bride. That dent and small chip in the corner allowed him to buy it from Big John's Appliances over in Dothan for half price. A hell of a deal and Mama could cook with just the flick of a knob.

I run my thumb over the exposed black indentation, my senses flooded with a stored whiff of my mama's gardenia perfume, the feel of her soft white apron between my fingers, can almost, almost hear her voice telling me to set the table, suppers near bout ready. Uncle Walter comes up behind me, breaks the spell with his big hands on my shoulders.

The scarred wooden table still sits cockeyed and off center in the big room, its two rounded-backed chairs set so that both Uncle and myself could watch the sun come up each morning in the east facing window over the sink and catch the day's last rays through the backdoor which we kept open except on the coldest of evenings.

The rooster and hen made in China still sit in the middle of the table, the arch of the roosters tail feathers still crooked. The blue plastic napkin holder in the shape of a fan, the one I bought for Mother's Day at Longstreet pharmacy, is right where it belongs, white paper napkins, folded double, rounded hump up, to the left of the rooster and hen.

Some little time after my mama died, I'm not sure how long exactly, time during those days moved around and past me, what I do remember clearly is sitting at that table, the ceramic rooster cupped in my child's hands. My hands, fingernails always just a little dirty at the edges in those days, I can still see them cradling that keepsake of my mamas.

That day I heard my mama's voice as clear and bright and true as a winter morning, "Ever'body needs some little bit a pretty around em."

I could see her, not a vision exactly, but real, solid, as if I had passed into a parallel world where she was still alive, still my mama, not some lifeless doll woman in a wooden box or an angel up in heaven where I couldn't get at her. Watching her image there in the dust motes of the morning sun I was thinking on the day she brought home those decorations.

She unwrapped the rooster and hen from their newspaper nest, polished them with a dish towel, placed them in the center of that scarred wooden table. Her smile was so rare and yet so beautiful when it appeared that it could change your whole world. She smiled that day. The little lines at the corners of her mouth disappearing.

"Ever'body needs some little bit a pretty around 'em."

I threw the rooster before I suspected I could do such a thing. Watched it turn end over end twice and a half turn more before it hit the back door and fell in pieces onto the worn linoleum. When Uncle Walter came in from feeding the animals, I was sitting on the kitchen floor, the remains of the rooster gathered in a pouch of my cradled t-shirt. Uncle helped me up, gently placed the pieces of colored ceramic on the kitchen table, and together we glued the 'pretty' into a slightly lopsided version of its original self.

Today I am overcome with a feeling of having stepped, not into a kitchen, but into a time machine made up, not of flashing lights and magic crystals or sleek polished metal, but of 99 cent store relics, cupboard doors with grooves worn below the wrought iron handles and white eyelet curtains that billow ghostlike with each breeze. My inclination is to sink down into childhood. The years I've spent away from here as a grown, independent woman, are gone in a heartbeat, vanishing in one deep musty breath of my childhood home.

The sensation lasts only a moment, but it rocks me, makes me reach out for Julio, lean against the counter for support. My hand fluttering upward from my side gets no further than my waist before Julio is there, his warm arm around the small of my back, grounding me in the here and now.

Uncle Walter offers tea and I gratefully lower myself into a kitchen chair. My chair. The one with puppy teeth marks on both lower rungs. Uncle serves the tea in the pink tinted glasses I won at the county fair when I was eleven shooting tin rabbits that popped up in painted grass. The most expensive glassware in the house. I blew an entire months babysitting money before finally giving up on the purple lava lamp and cashing in my chips for a complete set of these made-in-Japan cut glass tumblers.

The tea is ice cold and so sweet it makes my teeth hurt a little. Perfect.

"I understand your mama is going to be visiting us," Uncle says to Julio in his formal, talking to the pastor after the service voice.

Julio tells Uncle that he'll be driving Aunt Ruth's Volvo up to Atlanta to pick up his mother tomorrow. I will not be going as I have the handy excuse of having to be out at the Bessie Smith Park for rehearsals for the talent contest which, along with a preview of the Strutting Your Stuff portion of the program will be taking place the following day.

This rehearsal is really about the Aunties having veto power over how much skin the contestants are showing and keeping the hip thrusts to a minimum in the talent competition. Since all I'm going to be doing is walking across the stage in my favorite jeans and a purple Hanes t-shirt followed by a demonstration suitable for public television, I could have easily talked my way out of this rehearsal. But that hardly seemed fair to the other contestants was my thinking once I learned that The Sainted Mother would be invading my sovereign state at the very same time as these rehearsals were scheduled.

By the time we've finished our tea I'm feeling like myself again, my grown adult self and I take Julio upstairs to show him my old room. My college text books are on wooden shelves along the wall opposite the bed, but other than that the room looks the same as it did when I slept here. Same yellow and rose pinwheel quilt on the twin Birdseye maple bed. Same tiny daisies on the open curtains. Same view of the hickory tree and the barn with Hunley Mountain a soft blue frame in the background. My collection of birds' nests and broken eggs, the outsides porcelain blue or speckled brown and cream, still line the dresser top. Hawk feathers and assorted rocks, a stuffed armadillo (my first project that long ago summer at the taxidermy shop) and pressed wildflowers sit side by side with early sketches of birds and plants, bugs and butterflies.

"This room it is nothing like the rooms of my sisters," Julio says as he fingers a jagged hunk of sparkling granite.

"No? You were expecting pink and glitter. My Little Ponies and Beanie Babies?"

His smile takes my breath away.

"No hardly," he says and he wraps his arms around me. "For me, this pinkneck room, this is right, no? Pinkneck?"

He's teasing and I bite his neck gently to show him I understand he's making fun of me.

"Your room when you were a child, it is very beautiful. Like you. Full with curiosity and love of life. It shows to me that you were a little girl of much intelligence and gusto for the world around you. Same like now, yes? A little pinkneck girl who is now a beautiful redneck woman."

Never in all the days and nights I spent growing up in this room did I imagine myself married to a man like Julio. A man not from around here. A man whose culture and language are not mine. A man with whom I plan to live, at least part of each year, in another country, away from everything I knew up until a few years ago. And yet, it seems to me that I am more complete with this Panamanian man than I could ever have been with a homegrown boy. My horizon reaches beyond Hunley Mountain and Martin's Ridge. My home is now with Julio and while I will always be a Noisy Creek girl, just thinking of the narrowness of my life without him causes my heart to ache, my breath to catch a little and my arms to tighten around his solid waist.

Preston Yates has done a bang up job of publicizing the Redneck Goddess Contest. Goggins Barbeque is filled to overflowing with locals and tourists alike, all smooched together along picnic table benches, their hands and faces streaked with smudges of reddish brown sauce. The shouted greetings when we step through the double door brings a TV crew from Atlanta up off their bench, hoping for an interview with one of the contestants.

Willy Goggins comes out from the kitchen, drying his hands on the front of his apron, the one with the decal of the surprised pig on the bib. He leads Uncle Walter and Julio through the kitchen, out the back door and onto a tiny covered patio set with a folding table and four chairs. I stay and quote Jeff Foxworthy to the reporters. Tell them a redneck woman can smoke a cigarette, drive a stick shift and nurse a baby all without spilling her beer. While they're still writing I escape through the swinging door of the kitchen and find Julio and Uncle Walter out back where the Goggins family take their meals.

From the kitchen I watch the two men through the smudged backdoor window. I have my cell phone in my hand even as I hug the neck of Wiley's wife, Mable.

"Aunt Snickers. What the hell? We're at Goggins and the place is full of news people. I don't see anybody national but Jimmy Morgan from WKXB up in Atlanta is here. How much publicity is this thing getting anyway?"

Aunt Snickers even sighs with a drawl.

"Honey, I just have no control over this. Preston knows folks. Folks that own TV and radio stations."

My own sigh is tinged with Latin accents, a sort of drawn out ieeeeey. "Auntie maybe it's because I've been gone a while, or I suppose it might be that, with Julio here, I'm more aware of how we look to outsiders, but, all families are odd. Funny and loving, but odd to outsiders. I just don't want a bunch of Yankees coming in here and making us out to be fools by only seeing a slim portion of what we really are."

"Goo Goo, all I can tell you is that I am doin' my best to take care that doesn't happen."

I steal a sweet potato fry on my way past Wiley and join the men on the back porch. We won't be bothered by reporters out here. Willy Goggins weighs well over four hundred pounds and makes a fine deterrent but it's Mable, ninety eight pounds of sinewy muscle wielding a foot long cleaver that will kill any desire on the part of the reporters to trespass through her kitchen.

When I join Julio and Uncle Walter, a pitcher of amber, a thin layer of foam half way down showing that the men have started without me, is on the bare table. I've interrupted the two of them and there's an awkward silence as Julio pulls out the rusty folding metal chair and I take my seat.

"I am saying to your Uncle Walter that I love you," Julio fills me in, "and making him an assurance that I will take care of you.

I wish I had stayed a mite longer with the pushy reporters and given the two of them more time to have this discussion without me.

Uncle Walter drinks his beer, sits with one shiny boot crossed over the opposite knee, studies Julio for a good long time, eventually gets to the heart of things.

"Is there gonna be trouble where you come from, you marryin' a white gal?"

To resist the urge to jump in, explain, argue, rescue Julio, I scoot my chair away from the table. Separate myself from these two, let them have at it.

"It is the same like here," Julio says. "Some people they do not approve that I do not marry a Panamanian woman, someone I have gone to school with, someone who is known by my family, someone who is more like me. But to these people I say only that I love Georgia Ginny Barr and they must do with this whatever is their will. I give to you my word of honor that no one will do any harm to this woman and that those people who are not able to accept her as my wife will have no part of our life together."

Uncle Walter stiffens a bit, his eyes squint into the distance. Willy brings plastic baskets lined with wax paper and heaped with pulled pork sandwiches, French fried sweet potatoes, and cold slaw.

Into the smell of mayonnaise, vinegar and grease, Uncle asks, "You got enough money to take care of my girl?"

"Yes sir," Julio assures Uncle. "Money it is not, how you say, an issue."

I dig into my sandwich and the men follow my lead after a few more seconds of staring at each other. I can't help but think of two male howler monkeys meeting in the treetops, posturing, testing each other's strength, assuring that each know where the line is drawn between territories.

"You goin' after that buck up on Martin's Ridge for that contest on Saturday?" Uncle asks between bites.

"Yeah. I'm gonna track him. Don't know if I'll take the shot. Seems a shame to kill him just for some silly contest."

"Up to you. Be careful up there. Watch out for that ole bear."

Julio, the only one who hasn't yet dived into the food greasing his waxed paper plate, looks up at this warning.

"This place where you will go, it is the same where you meet the bear?"

"Well," I hedge, "it's a big mountain, but yeah. Same basic area."

"This is a bad thing, yes?" Julio appeals to Uncle Walter.

"I don't like it any better'n you do son, but not a soul asked for my opinion."

"Oh stop it both of you! I've hiked those woods since I was in grade school. I'll have a rifle and a cell phone and some kind of GPS system attached to my waist. Something Preston Yates' insurance insisted on. I'm not going to be in any danger."

A vision of the underside of that charging bear, the crooked scar like a jagged bolt of lightning across her chest, flashes across my eyes, makes my heart do a little hippity hop and my palms sweat. Well. Lucky for me I don't believe in premonitions.

Chapter Thirteen

The Burnett twins are first up at the rehearsal. Our instructions are to sashay the length of the bandstand, turn and walk back so that the judges can get a good look at our backsides. Then we are to pose ourselves in the classic beauty contestant pose—one knee bent, head thrown back, a smile as big as our vanity. Gloria and Gladys are wrapped in tan trench coats which they are refusing to remove until the strut begins. Aunt Snickers and Aunt Ruth have given up explaining to them that there are no judges present today, this is only a practice and a preview to assure that the talent and costumes won't get anyone arrested for public nudity or, worse, offend any of the Baptist who will be in attendance. Aunt Snickers has said she wants the contest to reflect family values so many times I'm beginning to think I'm at a Jerry Falwell revival.

Still, it could be worse. I could be in Atlanta picking up The Sainted Mother. We're all going to dinner tonight over at The Plantation House. I had hoped to limit the guest list to immediate family, though in Noisy Creek that generally means only second and third cousins, but have given up even that restriction as a lost cause. I know Uncle Earl and Uncle Neil are coming because Uncle Earl called this morning to let me know he had 'checked with that feller over at that there restaurant and, so long as I wear a tie with my Dickies, he's fine and dandy with my a-tire.' My plan to get through the evening is called I believe disassociation, a sort of out of body experience that will allow me to view the entire meal as though I am watching a movie. I only hope it's a comedy and not a tragedy.

Here we go. Gladys and Gloria drop their coats like awkward strippers and the fun and games have begun here at The Bessie Smith Memorial Park rehearsal for The Redneck Goddess Contest. I myself am impressed with their creativity. They are wearing denim, though you have to look closely through the red, white, and blue sequins to see it. The idea of short shorts has cross bred with your basic G-string. Which, frankly wouldn't be so bad if the twins had availed themselves of a nice bikini wax at Aunt Ruth's spa before donning the outfits. They've tied torn white t-shirts under their uplifted boobs. Thin and, I'm pretty sure, wet t-shirts. From the look of them I'm guessing those shirts are glued on. The Aunties are so shocked that the twins actually get all the way across the stage and half way back before a halt is called to their promenade.

Aunt Ruth's voice comes out as a squeaky hinge, high and thin.

"For the love of God and all the angels, what were you girls thinking?"

Aunt Snickers has taken the more direct approach. She hurries up the steps of the bandstand and throws the trench coats back over their near naked bodies.

The twins stand dejectedly, their coats clutched closed, while Aunt Snickers and Aunt Ruth confer. Finally, after phrases like 'shocked near half to death' and 'never been so disappointed in all my born days' have floated out over our heads for a few minutes, Aunt

Snickers asks if anyone else intends to show their bee-hinds and titties to God fearin' people who have come to see a contest to determine the glory of southern womanhood. When, by a show of hands, it is revealed that about two thirds of us do indeed intend to show off our best assets up on that stage, the Aunties send us all home for four hours to come up with costumes that will leave something to the imagination.

Which gives me the day off. I find Aunt Ruth and assure her that I will be wearing my favorite jeans, a perfectly normal, not too tight or too thin, t-shirt, the appropriate undergarments and my red converse tennis shoes.

"Good Lord Goo Goo," Aunt Ruth says, "you could put yourself out a little bit."

"I intend to wash and comb my hair," I tell her and she shooes me away with the back of her fluttery hand.

"You know what I'm doing for my talent," I call back over my shoulder. "I'll see what the other goddess wanna-bes are up to the same time the judges see it tomorrow."

"The Plantation House at 7:00," she reminds me. "Don't you dare chicken out and leave the bunch of us there entertaining your future mother-in-law."

With a free day I decide to spend some time with Uncle Walter, but when I call he is in the truck on his way to Dothan to pick up a part for the Harvester.

"Y'all know where the key is," he tells me, "Go on over if'n you want. I'll be back a little past dinner time."

On the drive over to the house, a flock of Red Winged Black birds rises up out of the mist of Clayton's Slough. The birds turn in a swirl and disappear back into the cattails. The radio says rain is headed our way but right now the sun is turning the ground fog a shimmering gold and the day is ripe with promise.

Once I turn off rural route four, the road behind me is thick with red dust until I pull into the gravel drive that circles the house. I swing out of the truck, my Olympus hanging from my hand. I'm hoping for some good shots of the front porch. General Lee the fourth or it might be the fifth, lifts himself from his blanket and deems to give two half-hearted barks before returning to his interrupted nap.

I squat on the bottom step and aim the shutter at two pine chairs, the planks worn under their rockers. Shifting my butt on my heels, I capture a crate turned on end between the chairs, Uncle's yellow coffee mug abandoned on its slightly indented top. Between the cracks of the porch I spot a doodle bug weaving its zigzagging path through the dry dirt under the house.

"Doodle bug, doodle bug, fly away home," I whisper remembering summer days as a toddler hiding from the heat under this house, days when Mama was busy with one of the hundred chores that seemed to make up her day, "your house is on fire and your children will burn," I finish before coming up onto the porch.

I point the camera at General Lee, frame the ragged plaid blanket to the side of the largest rocker, General Lee curled in a ball. It's a study in muted colors that's a fact–the blanket faded maroon, navy and dirty white, the brown and white dog with his stubby tail touching his blunt black nose. The mid-morning sun creates a labyrinth of shadows filtering through the passion vine trailing thick along the eaves, brown and bare now but holding a gift of rich purple blooms come Spring.

I'm on a fools errand to capture the ghosts of a thousand moments of shared life I enjoyed here with Uncle Walter. Time has a way of flying past when I'm looking at it through the eye of the camera so that when I hear Uncle's Chevy pull into the yard, I'm shocked to see that it's almost 2:00. I have some good shots of the porch, the sun having cooperated and given me a soft pale yellow light for most of the morning. The shadows of the memories created here over the years may or may not show up when I print out these photos, but I know for a fact I'll be carrying them in the center of who I am for the rest of my life.

"Bet ya didn't eat," Uncle says as he climbs out of the truck, paper bag in hand.

"How well you know me. What you got there?"

"Ham and cheese sandwiches and a couple hunks a fresh blackberry pie from Rebs."

"Give me five minutes to clean up. I am starving now that I think of it."

Uncle makes a pot of coffee and we sit at the kitchen table. It'll spoil my appetite for supper tonight out at The Plantation House, but I don't expect to have much of a desire to eat anyway, so I go ahead and dig in.

I'm four bites into my sandwich when Uncle asks, "You 'member when you broke your arm?"

I chew a while, trying to see where he's going with this.

"I remember. You finished your sandwich already?"

"Lock stock and barrel," he nods. "You 'member me warning you about that horse?"

I nod, keep working on my ham and cheese.

"Nothin' would do but that you run over there the minute my back was turned and hoist yo'self up on that big ole thing. That horse was eighteen hands high and as green as spring grass, but you was determined to ride it."

"I remember. How old was I do you think? Twelve or so?"

"Lord child, you was a itty bitty thing. Couldn't a been no mo than nine or ten."

"Diablo," I say as I pick up the second half of my sandwich. "That was his name. I haven't thought of that horse in years. He was a beautiful animal wasn't he?"

Uncle stares at me. I know what he's saying here. But I'll be darned if I'm going to give him the satisfaction of admitting it.

I've finished my sandwich and am looking forward mightily to enjoying my pie before Uncle shakes his head and allows himself a lopsided grin.

"Stubborn as a darned Missouri Mule," he judges me before asking, "You get along all right with his mama?"

"Julio's her only son. Six younger sisters. He's been raised as the heir apparent. Did I tell you he was Bachelor of the Year in Panama?"

"Huh. So his mama thinks highly of him?"

"That's one way to put it, yeah. His family has always thought he'd go into politics. Not Julio's choice, but he'd have done it if he hadn't met me. With a gringa wife, he has no future in Panamanian politics. Truthfully, even if he was marrying a Spanish princess, I doubt his sainted mother would be ready to turn loose of him."

"Ah yeah. I know how she feels."

I wipe the blackberries from my mouth and kiss his cheek.

"Uncle Walter." My voice comes out soft, a child's plea instead of the adult's request I planned. "I love this man like crazy, but I'm about half scared to death my choosing him is gonna cost me your love."

Uncle looks as if I've struck him, "Child! How could you think such a thing?"

I lean across the scarred surface of that kitchen table and hug his neck for the moment that he'll allow it.

"Why ain't you out at the park practicing for that there Redneck deal?" he asks as I pretend not to notice when he wipes his eyes with a paper napkin.

I give him a censored version of the morning's events.

"Don't surprise me much them Burnett twins," he gossips. "Me and your daddy went to school with their mama and aunties. They was always right popular them Burnett gals."

The Sainted Mother will be staying with Julio and me. I hold this against God who promised to answer my prayers. We have a lovely Bed and Breakfast in Noisy Creek, but Senora Monterey relayed through Julio that, since she was traveling all this way to meet my family, she wanted to spend as much time as possible with me as well. How very special. I can hardly object what with Julio eating grits, nearly becoming gator bait, being shit on by a large startled bird, dumped in brown lake waters and having to swim for his life—all without losing his smile or becoming even a little grumpy. It is time for me to be as gracious with his family as he has been with mine. I doubt I have it in me.

I make it home in time to shower and change into an espresso colored cashmere shift. Simple and elegant with a deep V neck that demonstrates my affinity with the Burnett twins.

The dress belongs to Aunt Ruth and when she handed it to me yesterday her exact words were, "I'm beggin' you Goo Goo, wear it to dinner at The Plantation House with Julio's mother. If I see you in faded jeans and an old T-shirt one more time I swear I'm going to lose my ever-loving mind."

The shoes are suede and I find them on the front porch in a brown grocery bag when I get home from Uncle Walter's. They come with a no nonsense note— 'No. Your brown converse tennis shoes do not go with that cashmere dress. Wear these.'

The Volvo pulls into the driveway at just after 5:00. I've put new sheets in the guestroom, plush new towels in the bath and I've even arranged a tray of crackers and cheese on one of Auntie's beautiful silver trays. For the love of God I put a doily on the tray before fanning out the Ritz crackers. What more can I do?

I open the door wide in welcome and go out to help with the luggage. Julio opens the passenger door for his mother and offers his arm to escort her from the car to the house. Good Lord, it's twenty feet of level paving, not the wilds of Backwoodsville, but she clings to his arm and gazes around as if this entire experience is simply too much for a soul as delicate as hers. I haven't decided yet how to greet her. I'm so glad you're here is a big fat lie. Good to see you again, ditto.

I settle on, "How was your flight?"

I needn't have agonized over the greeting. She ignores me completely and opens with, "I did not realize you lived in the middle of the woods. I understand so much better now why you prefer your jungle butterflies to actual people."

I remind myself that the first words my wonderful Julio heard from my Uncle Walter were, "Who's that nigger with his hands on our girl?"

I swallow the retort that sits on the tip of my tongue and try for understanding and confident acceptance. The Queen Mother and I do our usual dance around the required air kiss greeting, both of us managing to avoid coming any closer than three inches from any part of the other. Once inside even Senora Monterey can't find fault with Aunt Ruth's home.

"This is lovely," she says in surprise. "Who decorated it dear? I'm sure it wasn't you."

"Mother," Julio breaks in, allowing me to swallow my answer along with the blood leaking from the tip of my tongue. "Perhaps a nap before supper would improve your disposition," he says in rapid Spanish.

Mama has an answer but it's too fast for me to follow though I'm pretty sure I catch the drift just fine. I'm not sure what the Spanish word for disrespectful whippersnapper is, but I bet it's in there somewhere. Julio winks at me over the top of his mother's head and leads her down the hall and into the guestroom. When he returns, the two of us carry in eight pieces of luggage which explains who taught my lovely fiancé the art of packing. The luggage takes up pretty much the entire floor space in the small guestroom. The Sainted Mother reclines on the bed while we make the five trips necessary to get it all inside.

As we're tiptoeing out of the room she calls sleepily, "Julio dear, have the girl come in an hour to begin the unpacking and to help me with dressing for our early dinner."

"Mother," again with the lightening fast Spanish, "we spoke of this. There are no servants."

"I'd be happy to help you unpack," I lie through my clenched teeth.

"That would hardly be helpful dear," she replies and Julio grips my arm firmly and leads me out of the room, shutting the door gently behind him.

We escape to our room where he scoops me up in his arms and carries me laughing toward the bed.

"You I miss all the day. I am like the fat white bread without the honey," he's nuzzling my neck and I have already forgotten The Great Resting Beast down the hall, "like the giant catfish without the whiskers." We're on the bed now, his silly words coming between soft quick kisses. "Like the grits without the butter."

"That's enough," I giggle, my breath quickening, my body already arching up to meet his. "Lock the door."

An hour later Julio is stepping from the shower, preparing to dress and wake his mother for our supper at The Plantation House. I'm tangled in the sheets, still naked and content. When I stretch and yawn and prepare to get in the shower his throaty voice comes to me from across the room where he's buttoning his silk shirt.

"Stop. Remove not the sheet until I am gone. Or we will be late to the dinner and my Sainted Mother will disinherit my besotted butt."

He says this to me in soft Spanish and I'm being loose in the translation of besotted. Horny might actually be a more accurate translation of the word. Either way I know he's speaking the truth and I follow directions, though I am sorely tempted to do a recon by boobies. I happen to know this move will draw fire every single time. Even in linen slacks and silk shirt with Mama just down the hall, this man can be locked and loaded in under five seconds.

I admit our love making had a touch of winning a competition with his mother in it for me. It feels a bit perverted but it's as old as Eve and whatever buxom lass Cain brought home. The wife may never be able to love the man as completely, as selflessly as his mama, but she wins his attention because she's the one with whom he's having sex, and sex trumps everything. Not my rules, that's just the way God made it. Watching Julio slip on his shoes, thread his belt through his pant loops, I have a flash of understanding that I will someday be on the other side of this cycle. Someday, our son, Julio's and mine, will choose some girl unworthy of his cherished attention, and he will leave me for her.

"You look like the cat that swallows the little parrot," Julio says as he finishes dressing and kisses my cheek.

"The canary. And I was thinking that it really was very nice of your mother to come all this way to meet my family. She loves you very much. Is only frightened for your happiness."

He sits on the side of the bed and I snuggle against his thigh while he brushes my hair off my forehead.

"Yes. Like your Uncle Walter. She is afraid because I do not choose the same path that she had chosen. Do not follow the road she has seen for me."

I'm slipping the required uniform of the evening over my head when my cell phone rings. The cashmere is silk lined and sensuous against my skin.

It's Aunt Ruth on the phone and I assume she's calling to make sure I am dressed properly and will be on time for the dinner.

"Hey," I tell her. "You're right. This dress does feel better than jeans and a Hanes."

"I'm glad Dear. Don't forget the shoes your Aunt Snickers sent over. Now let me speak with Margarita please."

"What? Margarita? How do you know...?"

"Goo Goo Honey, please. Just give your little phone to Julio's mother so I may speak with her a moment."

I find Julio and his mother in the living room. 'Margarita' is sipping a Cuba Libre from a tall frosty glass and Julio has a long neck bottle of Miller in one hand and a Ritz cracker stacked with cheddar in the other. When I announce that my Aunt Ruth is on the line for her, his mother smiles and accepts the phone as if she's been anticipating this delightful call. Julio follows me back down the hall while I finish dressing, leaving his mother to speak in private.

"How do my Aunt Ruth and your mother know each other?"

"They speak before," Julio says as though this is not important news that someone sure as heaven should have thought to mention to me before right this moment.

Upon further interrogation, Julio reports that he gave his mother's phone number to Collin a week or so ago.

"Your Aunt Ruth, she speaks with my mother. To welcome her to the family."

"Huh."

On the surface this phone acquaintance seems innocent enough, but it makes me nervous as a hog on the first frosty day of winter. It probably doesn't mean much, the farmer sharpening his knives next to that giant pot of boiling water, but, like the hog, I'm rolling my eyes a bit and casting about for an escape route.

The Plantation House is the most elegant restaurant within a hundred miles of Noisy Creek. Ok. It's the only restaurant within a hundred miles that has linen on the tables and serves a few items that aren't deep fried. Before the War of Northern Aggression it was owned by the Morgan family. My Aunt Ruth knows the history of the place. Her friend LuAnne who manages the beauty salon part of her spa, her family were slaves right here on this plantation. It's a local joke that the Morgans have all gone, died off or moved up north, but the descendents of the slaves are mostly still here. One of them, LuAnne's cousin Foley, is our current mayor.

The Plantation House is owned now by a corporation out of Atlanta. It started as a Bed and Breakfast with the restaurant sort of tacked on as a way to bring in some money during the off season but since the arrival of Chef Joshua Clark a few years ago, it has become the place to come for special dinners. Recently the gardens have been renovated and, according to Aunt Ruth, the place is now hosting outdoor weddings and anniversaries. I've never been to dinner here, though as a teenager Samuel and I and the usual group of miscreants did jump the fence and party in an old gazebo out back one summer night.

Tonight the convoy instructions, as usual, became slightly confused at the last minute. Aunt Ruth and Collin swung by and picked up Senora Monterey for reasons which are still not clear to me. While Julio and I were ordered out to the back of beyond to rescue Uncles Earl and Neil who had intended to arrive together but were having trouble getting Uncle Earl's truck started and had requested a ride.

By the time we pull into the grassy field off to the left where we are directed to park, every live oak has vehicles parked in its mossy overhang. Julio pulls up in front to let me off but the Uncles raise such a fuss about me being too ladylike suddenly to walk across a field that I finally insist that he just park the damn car in the grassy lot.

Evidently Uncle Earl's original idea of wearing a tie with his Dickies has been vetoed by the Aunties. Both

Uncles are dressed in black trousers, long sleeved cotton shirts that still bear the store creases and wide clip on ties they must have had in the back of their closets since the fifties. Uncle Earl's striped collar still had a round headed pin protruding from it when we arrived to pick them up. Both men have the white necks of those newly shorn at Oliver's Barber shop. I barely recognized the two of them, like their appearance much better in ratty overalls and stained ball caps, an opinion I keep to myself since they've obviously gone to a lot of trouble to look presentable for my soon to be mother-in-law.

Julio, already scandalized by not letting me off in front of the restaurant the way every well brought up young prince is taught to do, eyes my suede shoes when he opens my door and simply picks me up in his arms and carries me across the burr infested lot. Now I know that little bitty girls probably get this kind of thing all the time. But I haven't been a little girl since my fifth birthday. I'm not only tall, but no one has ever described me as small boned. Barr women are full bosomed, long waisted, and wide hipped. My older Aunties fall into two categories. Those like my Aunts Ruth and Snickers who exercise and diet themselves to near fixation or those who steam through the world like stately cruise ships covered in flowered rayon. So a man who thinks nothing of scooping me up in his arms and carrying me away, well he sweeps me off my feet in more ways than one.

By the time we arrive at the wide double doors of the old mansion, I am hanging on Julio as though he's the best thing since hawg jowls and black-eyed peas and the Uncles are grinning like house cats with guppy scales flashing from their teeth. The maitre´ de throws open the doors and the room before us explodes with the happy shouts of a surprise engagement party. I think I may be crying. I know I'm squealing and jumping up and down like a silly little girl.

The entrance hall is decorated for Fall in twinkling fairy lights and pyramids of pumpkins. A cut glass vase as big as a calf is filled to over flowing with hot house Tiger Lilies and African Daisies and some kind of curly sticks which have been sprayed gold and dusted with glitter. Dozens of candles in sconces on tables and walls and in sparkling orange and yellow votive holders give the room a near magic aura. In the center of all this glittering welcome is Senora Monterey standing between Aunt Ruth and Aunt Snickers, both of them with an arm around her waist, The Sainted Mother a sort of fully clothed ice sculpture between them.

Chapter Fifteen ★

In my time away from Noisy Creek I have forgotten how it feels to be in a room with over two hundred people, all of whom love and accept me, all of whom have gone to some trouble to make sure I know how delighted they are to have me in the family. That some of those present do not approve of my choice of fiancés is irrelevant. They're here, with smiles on their faces and champagne glasses in hand. Well, ok. In the case of most of the uncles they're hefting long neck bottles, but the point is the same.

Standing here in this elegant room, the drawl of love all around me, I have an epiphany. These people, many of whom have never been out of Georgia, some have never been outside the county, they ask me repeatedly how I find the courage to live in a foreign country. The phrase I've heard the most since coming back is, 'Why I'd be scared near half to death. I don't know how y'all do it."

This right here. This love and pride in me and acceptance of who I am, this is how I do it. It's an interesting fact that the better a child is raised, the more likely she is to find her own path in the world, a path that may be very different from that of those people who loved and raised and now miss her.

It seems at first an odd choice of dates for an engagement party. The very day Julio's mother arrives, the night before the opening of The Redneck Goddess Contest. But as the evening progresses, I grow to increasingly respect Aunties Ruth and Snickers' understanding of human nature in staging the production now. This demonstration of the support of my untamed, loving family, it is antidote against the venom of The Sainted Mother at the same time it fills me with the confidence I need to slide the chip from my shoulder and accept Julio's mother on her own terms. By party's end, Margarita Monterey is dancing country swing with Uncle Neil and she has taught a swaying line of Aunties the salsa hip sway. The champagne is a strong lubricant, but mostly this big family of mine overpowers her reservations and sweeps her up into their fun. Julio and I, dancing a slow country waltz to George Strait, watch his mama with her hands on Uncle Walter's hips, doing her Latin best to loosen his farmer's joints and convince him to move a little to the music.

By midnight the party is breaking up amidst promises to see everyone tomorrow out at the park for the first day of the goddess contest. I fall asleep in the back seat on the ride home. When the alarm shatters my dreams of dancing through the sparkling air of the tropics, I cannot remember getting from the car to the bed. It's still dark but the alarm face swears it is indeed time to get myself up and ready for the day. Why oh why did I agree to participate in this contest?

The sky is clear blue as though Preston Yates has so much money he actually can control the weather. I'm driving Uncle Earl's truck, have left the Volvo for Julio and his mother. Driving across town sipping coffee I peer through the cracked windshield and analyze how this blue sky differs from the blue of the tropics. More manganese than cobalt I decide and paler, much paler.

It's the light that makes the difference. The northern sun here, making everything softer, less starkly revealed. I park the truck, wait the minute and a half it takes the old vehicle to register that I've turned off the ignition and then slide out the door into the crisp morning air to see what the day will bring.

The park is buzzing with young women hot for the money, the 4x4 and the glory of being declared the ultimate Redneck Goddess hereabouts. I didn't do girlie dress up parties as a child. I did go to my senior prom, but I went fishing with Uncle Neil in the morning and only just made it home in time for a quick shower before slipping on the simple dress I'd finally agreed to let Aunt Ruth buy me after four endless hours of shopping at some Atlanta Boutique mall to which she had drug me kicking and screaming and pouting.

This crisp morning a mist of estrogen and scented hair products permeates the air, mixes with the poison of nail polish and the chemical tinge of makeup. I much prefer the smell of swamp water and gator shit. Cassandra Hollywood flits through and around the action, directing the camera crew, skirting me and Lizzie Ragsdale, aiming her phallic eyed camera at my preening home girls.

Aunt Snickers buzzes my cheek in welcome as she rushes past me.

"You're number ten in the line-up Goo Goo. Do you need anything to set up?"

Before I can tell her that I'm wearing my outfit and my laptop is in the truck, she's off again, her gentile voice raised in frustration.

"Mary Beth, you are getting on my last nerve girl. I promise you I will sew a skirt on that outfit my own self if you don't stop that pulling at it so as to show more of your little butt."

By 9:00 the necessary body parts have been coated with Vaseline, temper tantrums and crying jags are over, hair has been lacquered and blow dried, and my aunties are worn to a frazzle. As the high school band strikes up Gretchen Wilson's Redneck Woman, the whole mess of us parade out on stage, our heads high, our tummies sucked against our straight spines. For me, the day has become surrealistic. Surely I am going to wake up momentarily from this dream of wiggling butts and bouncing boobies.

From my place on stage I look down to see Julio and his mother in the second row. Uncles Walter, Neil and Earl flank them on each side. Julio's smile of pride and amusement returns my soul to my body and I grin at him in collusion. Uncle Walter looks slightly embarrassed but he's clapping his calloused hands and smiling slightly. Uncles Earl and Neil are grinning like apes in a monkey house immediately after the shipment of bananas. Senora Monterey is once again stone cold sober, smiling stiffly and clinging to Julio's arm for protection from the natives.

Preston Yates struts onstage and rattles on for a few minutes explaining the contest rules. He brags about the park until half the audience is fidgety, talking to their neighbor or yawning. When Aunt Snickers rolls her fisted hands in the classic 'wrap it up' signal, he switches his topic to the glorious new statue of local Civil War hero Bessie Smith designed and created by his talented daughter Kristen which will be unveiled on the last day of the contest. The fact that the man says Civil War instead of War Between the States demonstrates once again that you can take the Yankee from up north but y'all are never gonna take the misguided attitude from the Yankee.

The lineup of contestants is bracketed by the Burnett twins on point and the Foster twins in the drag position. Once we've all paraded past the judges and spectators, we file off stage and Gloria and Gladys open the show with their talent demonstration. It's a great opening act even with the revisions on which the Aunties insisted. The Burnetts prance onstage from opposite ends. Their modified costumes of sequined red, white and blue cutoff jeans and white t-shirts tied under uplifted breasts are closer to CMT video than a strip club. Though it's a close call.

Their act opens with juggling a six pack of Budweiser back and forth between the two of them, moves into a bump and grind to the bass rhythms of Trace Atkins growling nonsense syllables in a voice dripping with sexual innuendo, and ends with some sort of dance on twin fireman poles that is quite frankly beyond my experience and sexy as all get out. The highlight occurs when one of the beer cans explodes and Gloria catches it in midair and giggles while the spray turns her t-shirt transparent.

When the girls bounce off stage I'm ready to concede the contest and have the whole bunch of us just go home.

This is not to be. The exciting opening act is followed by Mary Beth Goodin singing Tricia Yearwood's Georgia Rain while accompanying herself on guitar. Which, given that Mary Beth is drop dead gorgeous, her short shorts damned near reveal enough to prove she's a natural blonde, and her voice is reminiscent of cayenne spiced honey, turns out to be very entertaining indeed.

Cousin Peanut Barr, whose real name is actually Priscilla but under the circumstances prefers to go by the Barr nickname, is next up. Peanut is dressed in a soft denim skirt. Her only nod to the contest being the possible opening of one button more than normal on her pale blue collared blouse. This cousin has the darkest hair in the family, the color of mahogany, it flows in soft curves to her shoulders. With my unruly fire engine red curls, I've always been jealous of Peanut's glory. This morning, she elegantly lives up to the Barr name with a stirring rendition of General Lee's description of The Great Traveller, known to every Barr child over the age of five.

"If I was an artist like you," Peanut begins and every Barr in the park moves their lips right along with her, "I would draw a true picture of Traveller, representing his fine proportions, muscular figure, deep chest, short back, strong haunches, flat legs, small head, broad forehead, delicate ears, quick eyes, small feet, and black mane and tail. Such a picture would inspire a poet, whose genius could then depict his worth, and describe his endurance of toil, hunger, thirst, heat and cold; and the dangers and suffering through which he has passed. He could dilate upon his sagacity and affection, and his invariable response to every wish of his rider. He might even imagine his thoughts through the long night-marches and days of the battle through which he has passed. But I am no artist Markie, and can therefore only say he is a Confederate Gray."

As Peanut takes her bow, every ball cap in the park is held over a swelling heart. From my place off stage I can see Uncle's Earl and Neil as they surreptitiously touch paper bags of foaming breakfast in a heartfelt toast.

Patricia Ragsdale is next onstage, her demonstration of yoga poses explains why her boyfriend Fred always has a smile on his face. I watch awestruck as the girl puts both feet behind her head. Aunt Ruth catches up with me and insists on doing some sort of fluffing thing with my hair. She kisses my forehead when she's finished and proclaims me gorgeous as always and then it's my turn to show off my talent.

Once I got over my initial stage fright at my first high school debate meet, I found that I am one of those rare people who love being on stage. A psychologist friend told me that I am normally so quiet and introverted that on stage is the only time I let myself play in the presence of others. Nice theory, but I believe the real reason is that as a child, from the very first time I showed off a kindergarten stick figure drawing, a dozen relatives clapped their hands and patted my head and exclaimed over my absolutely amazing intellect and creativity. I would show up at an aunties in dirty jeans and an oversized sweatshirt clutching a clay snowman and the first words out of her mouth would be, 'Why Goo Goo, you get more beautiful every single time I see you. Come on in now and let me see this wondrous creation of yours. Y'all are just in time to help with these cookies."

So when I walk onstage and see my whole family spread out below, all of them smiling, most of them clapping, a few whistling and stomping and carrying on like striped assed apes, I grin like the Cheshire cat and commence with my talent demonstration. With a push of a button, the raw voice of Ray Charles singing *Georgia* floats out over the crowd. There are some in the park who remember when Mr. Charles was barred from performing up in Atlanta during the death throes of Jim Crow. The past is a funny thing. We all know we've gotta learn from it, but there ain't no way to do that without confronting our missteps.

While Mr. Charles croons, I make my laptop communicate with the wide screen that the Clark boys have already set up on the stage behind me. I've added the pictures of Uncle Walter's old house to my collection and I start the show off with the shot of the current General Lee flaked out in a spot of yellow sunlight on a worn porch step. I interject Noisy Creek landmarks into shots of local butterflies. It's all done with soft light, framing that leaves out any hint of harsh reality and ends up showing my home town as a little slice of southern heaven. Somewhere between a photo of The Confederate Soldier and an old shot of Uncle Walter kneeling beside a four pointer, Ray Charles gives way to the Georgia Mountain Men who sing the lullaby of The Bonnie Blue Flag. When I walk off stage, I doubt I've scored many points with the judges, but I'm thinking the chamber of commerce will be calling soon wanting use my carefully framed view of reality on their website.

By the time Patsy Foster has hit the final off key note of Southern Nights and the dust has settled from her twin Veronica's final cartwheel, it's well after dinner time. It's a credit to southern womanhood, if one cares to look at it in that light, that not one male has slipped away to the barbeque grills set up under the Chestnut tree. Young and old, them good ole boys stay for the last flash of boob and butt. Anybody swears the way to a man's heart is through his stomach is off by a good few inches.

Events are behind schedule and The Great Promoter is worried that the last contestants will be driving their jeeps through the muddy course in the dark. Klieg lights are being set up as folks suck the last sauce from ribs and balance the crinkled edges of stained paper plates to scoop up the final smidgen of slaw. I'm to be in the dead last group of four to negotiate the track. The last contestants through the mud will be Lizzie, the Burnett twins and me.

"That there Clark gal, Betty Lou, the one what done the knife throwin', I believe she done won that talent contest is what she done," Uncle Earl proclaims to a head shaking Uncle Neil.

"No such'a thing. T'were them Burnett twins what rightly dee-serve to win. That there ad lib of the gal on the right when that beer exploded? That was pure-dee talent is what that was.

Chapter Fifteen ★

I've joined my family for dinner. I figure mud will soon enough cover the glob of barbeque sauce that has already set on the breast of my purple t-shirt. Most of the other contestants are behind the sound stage retouching their make-up and fussing with their hair or else they've slipped up the trail and are settling themselves with a cold brew and a hot male. I myself would be in this latter group if I could unclench his mama's hand from Julio's muscular arm. All this attention and excitement has made me hotter'n a truck bed in July.

Both Auntie Ruth and Snickers have made it a point, even in the hullabaloo of choreographing sixteen unruly young hillbilly women and various venders, cooks, sound people and well-meaning relatives, to hug my neck and pronounce Senora Monterey 'good people'. If the judgment had come from almost anyone else I'd just chalk it up to there be no accounting for the taste of others. But when, over my second plate of ribs, Uncle Walter juts his sauce stained chin toward the folding chair that is serving as The Sainted Mother's throne and proclaims her to be a 'damn fine woman', well, about then I figure maybe I'll have another look see at my future mother-in-law.

Hard to believe but maybe I missed something. I suppose it's possible that I may have even taunted her a little with my rural ways. As I weave a path through the crowd with three tall plastic cups of sweet tea balanced precariously on a wet cardboard tray, I take my time, watch Julio and his mother through the moving frame of rednecks. Senora Monterey cannot keep her hands off her son. She strokes his arm. Brushes a dark wave of hair from his forehead. Julio is talking and from the wide movement of his hands, I'm guessing he's speaking in their native tongue. The look of adoration and devotion she is bestowing on him strikes me as that of The Madonna to her son, her savior, her God. That look right there, I gotta wonder if that might not have been the real reason Jesus never married.

The day which began clear and cloudless is becoming oppressively humid. Clouds are building over Martin's Ridge, increasingly darker layers topped with soft luminous gray and touching the tree tops with black as menacing and deep as the open barrel of a shotgun. When a shift in wind drops the temperature by ten degrees in the time it takes two hundred locals to glare at the sky and try and remember if they brought their jackets, the rain is less than ten minutes away.

Four Jeep Wranglers are ready to go, parked side by side in the shelter of the parks biggest sweet gum, the area cordoned off with hemp rope, waiting for the last competition of the day. The little 4x4's range from a camouflage 1991 that looks as though someone has taken a ball peen hammer to near about every square inch of the passenger side, to a 1987 flashy primer job tricked out with a home painted flame eating at the rust pocked hood. Beside the vehicles is a waist high metal table arrayed with a lug wrench, various screw drivers, ratchets and oily jeep parts. What isn't on that table is one of those handy blue plastic tarps to keep the mud off your ass as you lie under the jeep to fix what ails it.

By the time the first four contestants head for the parked jeeps, the rain is blowing sideways in a cold spray and half the audience has disappeared leaving instructions with those remaining kinfolk who are sheltering under the oaks.

"Y'all call and tell me if something exciting happens, you hear?"

I believe it is a fitting testimony to the enduring appeal of the combination of redneck women and mud that nearly every loyal fan left standing in the cold rain, their jackets held over their heads or water dripping from the brims of their caps, warming themselves with the contents of an aluminum can, nearly every single audience member is male. One of the few exceptions is Miss Cassandra and her little crew of helpers scurrying around like ticks on a wet dog.

An air horn calls the first four contestants to their positions just outside the braided rope. Ella May Clark, whose fire eating routine was a crowd pleasing display of rare talent, is first in line. Ella May, known since seventh grade as Chesty, is wearing a pair of cut off jeans that leave nary a thing to the imagination and a white t-shirt that, one can only presume, belongs to her six year old sister. Loralee Sinclair is beside her in a pair of Davis Overalls over a red sweatshirt the exact color as the cap on the bib's brand name monkey. Sue Ann Goodin is next in a pair of jeans so tight the girl hasn't taken a full breath since she laid flat on the floor and zipped them up in the make shift dressing room. Last in line and, forgive me, but least in brains is Ella May's cousin Cloris who is decked out in a denim mini skirt, platform heels and what appears to be a tea towel wrapped around her flat bosom so as to showcase her dragon tramp stamp.

"Can you explain to me this competition?" Senora Monterey asks. She and I are sheltering under a dark blue umbrella which Uncle Walter has fetched from his pick up.

No ma'am I don't believe I can.

"The main idea I suppose is that redneck women are self reliant. Able to take care of themselves."

"Also," Julio adds straight faced. "It is true, no? These cookies, they like a good time in the mud?"

I'd punch his arm, but his mother is between us.

"Crackers. Not cookies. And, in a way that's exactly correct. We ain't afraid to get dirty to have a good time."

To Uncle Walter who is standing beside me, hunkered down under his green John Deer cap I wager, "Ten bucks says Loralee Sinclair takes this round."

"Nope," his slow voice returns. "The rest a them gals has hobbled themselves. The gator killer's niece is gonna take this one."

Scanning the dripping crowd I spot Hugh Sinclair perched on a picnic table under a moss draped Live Oak. He lifts his foam wrapped beer can in salute, grins to let me know he sees me and drains the contents.

Preston Yates, from the protection of the covered grandstand, sounds an air horn and the women rush toward their jeeps. Loralee pops the hood first thing and checks the oil and water, fiddles with the spark plugs. The other three young women barrel into the driver's seats and attempt to crank up the vehicles. Two won't start at all, Cloris's jeep has a flat rear tire, though she doesn't notice this until she's bumped the vehicle through the mud a good twenty yards from the table of tools. It's hard to hear from here which engine coughs, which sputters and which isn't turning over at all.

Loralee is holding up the distributor cap in the flamed jeep, drying it on the belly of her sweatshirt. Ella May's near bare ass is still sticking out from under the hood of the ball peened jeep. Cloris is poking at the flat rear left tire and attempting to fix it the way she's always done before. She's looking helpless, hoping for rescue from a strong gullible male. Sue Ann has removed the fuel filter on her vehicle and she's mincing her way through the mud toward the tools and parts when Loralee, having successfully replaced the distributor cap tears out of the staging area to begin the course.

Loralee was a freshman up at Athens when I was a senior. We didn't hang out together much but I did show her around campus and I feel confident in saying that when she revs the engine, slips the clutch and slides the jeep sideways throwing red sloppy mud full frontal onto the dainty stepping Sue Ann, she does it on purpose.

The crowd roars its approval. From behind me I hear Uncle Neil give a rebel yell and shout out, "That there is a redneck woman!"

The course is tame, not meant to actually test the off-road driving skills of us country girls. Mud slinging and some mild skidding, that's all we're meant to do here. They've even hauled in gravel to firm up the creek crossing as though every last one of us hasn't floated sideways a time or two in a foolhardy attempt to cross a swollen creek or gotten stuck to the axle and had to dig and winch our way out. Loralee finishes the course in under ten minutes and then barrels through the finish line and heads for the spectators where she makes a couple of mudslinging circles around the beer drinkers, forcing them into a tight bawling herd.

Sue Ann is the next to start her engine having replaced the fuel filter in fury over Loralee's mud splattering. She accelerates in a tight circle around the remaining jeeps, coating Ellie May and Cloris with mud while laughing like a deranged ape. Unfortunately for Sue Ann, she displays more enthusiam than good sense. In her third trip around the circle, she takes the final turn too fast, slides the jeep sideways down a small grade, tries to recover by turning into the slide and hitting the gas and ends with the jeep sliding sideways in slow motion and landing on its passenger side ten feet from the open mouths of Uncle's Earl and Neil. Sue Ann is out of the vehicle and using some mighty un-Baptist language before Uncle Earl can swallow his mouthful of Jax.

I peek over at Senora Monterey and am surprised, nigh shocked is closer to the truth, to see a huge grin and a sparkle in her eyes that gives me some kind of hope that the two of us might yet mend our fences. While we wait for Cloris to change the tire and for Loralee to figure out what nearly everyone in the audience already knows judging by the slipping sound coming from under the hood of her jeep, I ask Julio's mother if she's enjoying herself.

"When I was young, we went each summer to the family finca on Volcan Baru. My father he had an old American Army jeep which he allowed my brother to drive. I was older, but being the girl, it was Anthony who always drove. I know not why but the battery in this roofless coughing vehicle was under the passenger seat. The mountain rain poured freely in and at each bounce sparks flew from under my butt as the battery made contact with the metal seat bottom. I am thinking now that perhaps my granddaughters will be the one's driving the jeep while their brother's are the ones with fire escaping from their bottoms."

Before the next group of four contestants lines up, Aunt Ruth calls an official time out and gathers us all under the covering of the grandstand. While the Gauthier Elementary school band plays what is either a slow version of Dixie or possibly a speedy America the Beautiful, Auntie reads us the riot act. No more horsing around! Thank Jesus Sue Ann or a spectator wasn't hurt! Contestants will be disqualified for unnecessary risk taking.

None of us is listening. I feel badly for Aunt Snickers, but what did she expect would happen if she gave beater jeeps to a bunch of mud loving rednecks and told them to go at it? Still that new Wrangler and the money is an incentive and the bunch of us calm down a smidgin'. At the moment I just want to get this over with and go home to soak my frozen body in Aunt Ruth's old claw foot tub.

The next two groups of four manage to replace cracked distributor caps, fix loose spark plug wires, change broken fan belts and water pumps, repair corroded battery cables, and change clogged fuel filters. By the time the Burnett twins, Lizzie and I are standing behind the rope listening to our instructions, the rain is a silver wall of shimmering cold and the crowd looks like the one in the bleachers the last inning of a t-ball game. We're behind you all the way gals but hey somebody catch that fly ball and put us all out of our misery.

I've borrowed a sweatshirt from Uncle Earl. Since it's fluorescent orange with a picture of Larry the Cable guy's ass hanging above his low rider jeans and the words 'Just say no to crack', I've chosen to wear it inside out. I'm also wearing Uncle Neils matching furry orange Elmer Fudd hat, with the ear flaps tightly tied under my chin. I've traded my sneakers for a pair of my nephew Riley's leather work boots. Lizzie, standing beside me in a V-neck purple t-shirt, has goose bumps as big as her nipples which are clearly exposed through the wet shirt. No one, though, is paying much attention to either of us. The Burnett twins are the hands down favorite in this last round of the day.

The girls are wearing matching flesh colored skin tight tank tops under cut off overalls. Before we lined up they staged a mud fight which has resulted in both of them and most of the male spectators looking like red clay coated chickens ready for the baking oven.

To Aunt Snickers reprimand they replied, all mock wide eyed innocence, "It weren't dangerous, just a little bit dirty."

Just the attitude the shivering die hards in the audience are looking for in a redneck gal. The crowd screams and stomps in the mud in its enthusiasm and support of the twins. Julio has returned from driving his mother to the house where one can only hope she is taking a nap and contemplating her glorious good fortune in her son marrying into this family.

When the air horn sounds, the twins slap each other on the ass and head for their assigned jeeps. Lizzie and I are already investigating our vehicles. All four resemble red mud pies on wheels more closely than they resemble conveyance of any kind. Mine has a flat front tire. No big deal to diagnose, but a muddy mess to fix. By the time I've wedged a concrete block into the mud to support the jack, I'm already covered in slick red goop. Might as well have worn the sweatshirt ass side out.

I'm tightening the last lug nut as Lizzie cranks up her jeep and eases onto the now very sloppy course. By the time I've got the jack out from under the vehicle, I can hear Lizzie's engine making that high pitched whine that means she's gotten that little jeep stuck up to the axle. The twins have finished together and before climbing behind the wheel are giving some sort of boob shaking, ass wiggling good bye to the roaring crowd. Yes indeed. These are my people.

We are, all of us glorious representatives of southern womanhood, well beyond caring about getting muddy at this stage. So when the twins rev the engines, slip the clutches and throw buckets of mud my way there's not much I can do but wipe the mud from my eyes like one of those pie faced comedians, grin and get behind the wheel. I hold my face up to the stinging rain, a mud coated goddess with wild red hair framing her Elmer Fudd hat, shivering cold and as happy as if I had good sense.

The course is slip sliding sloppy but it's the creek that has become the challenge. As I slide down the hill to its edge I can see Lizzie on shore, her jeep a few feet into the waters slipping slowly sideways in the current. The twins have tried to go around the course outlined crossing and both jeeps are now stuck up to the engine blocks. One resting against a boulder a few feet into the creek and the other sideways with its hood against the back bumber of its twin.

I get out and call down to my cohorts, "I believe we need a plan."

Lizzie and I walk the creek bank while the twins begin gathering rocks and tree limbs and whatever else they can find to give us some traction. About a half mile downstream the creek widens out before running through Bear Gorge and the normally trickling cascade called Old Man Falls. I think I can drive crosswise of the current and make it across that wide spot and to the other side. Once there I'll come upstream and we ought to be able to winch the other three jeeps across the rising creek. It's a plan. Time will tell if it's a good plan.

When Lizzie and I get back to the jeeps the crowd led by none other than Miss Hollywood and her crew is already there. I can see Collin holding a red umbrella over Aunts Ruth and Snickers while the two of them confer with a soggy Preston Yates. It looks like we're about to be shut down. Just when the fun was starting too. I climb in my jeep and, pretending not to hear the cries of my poor aunts, head downstream. I cannot be held to blame for the fact that I have no rearview mirror and just can't see them back there shouting and hopping up and down in the rich red mud.

The rain has stopped but the creek is still coming up. It's already a couple inches higher than when Lizzie and I scouted the crossing. If it's deeper than I think and the jeep gets swept toward the gorge, I'll swim for it. Otherwise I intend to roar across as fast as this old 4x4 will take me. That's my plan. That and a fervent prayer to Sweet Jesus that this not be the last dumb ass decision I make in my life.

I come down the bank in first gear the old engine's rev a sweet, high pitched whine that blocks the sound of all that rushing water. Two seconds in, the cold creek hits my ankles and I know I'm in trouble. Nothing to do now but gun it and see how far I get before my swim. A raven cracaws at my stupidy and the water is thick maroon soup flowing free across the floor board. Adrenaline and pride carry me to the creek's middle.

It ought to get easier from here except the left front tire hit's a gravel bar, the jeep slips sideways of the current and I'm a couple dozen yards closer to the gorge before I can get straightened out with the hood headed toward the far bank again. Having scared the devil out of me, the Good Lord now provides a lovely rocky high spot that takes me out of the current. Before I can say 'Thank you Jesus,' I am on the opposite bank, my heart pounding hot blood in my ears, a grin on my face as I head upstream to help Lizzie and the Burnett twins finish the race.

Arriving back at the course it's immediately clear that my aunts and Preston Yates have other plans. The twins are nowhere to be seen. Ditto for most of the male audience. My Aunties are still there and they do appear to have a plan. From the looks they give me across that rising creek I think this plan most probably involves shaking me until my teeth rattle before skinning me alive. The roar of the creek, the pounding of the rain which has returned to marry above us with ice clouds to produce buckshot hail—I simply cannot hear what my aunts are yelling across the swollen creek. I wave gaily from my side of the creek and head for the finish line.

Chapter Sixteen

Dawn is a shimmering promise of blood red in the eastern sky as I start up Martin's Ridge. The frozen ground crunches with each step, the air too cold to carry the smell of the pines or the musk of the dead hickory and hackberry leaves through which I crunch. My throat aches with each frozen breath. Weighted with rope and a small pulley, a GPS tracking device and flashlight, bottles of water and a box of granola bars, the pack pulls me off center. The cracked leather strap of my bolt action Winchester .30-06 is already rubbing a sore spot on the front of my left shoulder. The pockets of my old down hunting jacket hold ammo, my antler handled buck knife and the razor sharp hook nail skinning tool I've carried since my summer job at Uncle Nuggie's taxidermy shop.

I'll be achy sore with a blister or two by nightfall and call it a fair trade for this time alone in what's left of the wilderness I've roamed and tramped since I was old enough to sneak off on my own. My hope is to be at the crest of the ridge by full dawn. From there I'll work my way around to the high meadow, settle myself against the scaly bark of a Hickory and, if the buck shows up, I'll decide whether to take the shot. If the big guy doesn't show, well I've had me a fine day in the late Autumn woods.

My noisy, early morning passing has interrupted the sleep of a flock of Eastern Jays. They rise as one from the bare bones branches of a dying oak making enough noise to wake the dead. The first warning system of the forest, their indignation echoes through the trees letting every wild thing within five miles know some redneck with a gun is in the territory.

Weaving through the trees, doing my best to be as quiet as possible for a hundred and thirty pound animal loaded down with enough gear to slow a mule, I have plenty of time to replay the events of last night. More time really than I'd like. Aunties Ruth and Snickers both spoke with me on the phone.

'What were you thinking?' and 'Do you have any idea what might have happened crossing that creek by yourself like that?" were the dominant themes delivered in tones of anger and disappointment over my flawed decision making abilities.

It was Julio though who made me just a little ashamed of myself. He folded my mud covered body into his chest, nearly squeezed the life out of me and whispered into my ear.

"You are no more allowed to be foolhardy with your life."

I had my big mouth open to inform him that he was not now and never would be the boss of me. I was going to tell him exactly that just as soon as he released me and the breath came back into my chest. But when I looked up at him and saw the tears pooling in his dark eyes, my throat closed on the words and I only nodded my head against his chest and hoped he'd turn me loose before breaking any of my ribs.

Once home I stayed in the old claw foot tub for over an hour, adding hot water so that the steam turned the bathroom into a rendition of Panama in August. Then I put on my comfortable gray sweats which I had luckily rescued from Uncle Walter's Goodwill pile, stuck my feet into those gray and red wool socks that old ladies use to make sock monkeys, made myself a mug of hot chocolate laced with Southern Comfort and joined Julio and his mother.

Walking into the living room I felt as if I had entered one of those 'What's Wrong with This Picture' puzzles on the back page of those Highlight magazines. Julio's mother was arranged in Aunt Ruth's mauve recliner. Her silk pajamas and matching robe creating a soft frame the color of Dom Perignon. Her salt and pepper hair swept up into a loose French roll, her legs crossed ladylike at her trim ankles, from where I stood even the soles of her matching slippers appeared elegant. Julio was lounging on the love seat beside her wearing a matching pajama and robe set which The Sainted Mother must have carried with her from Panama. A gift for the Prince. Both were sipping martinis complete with cocktail onions and stuffed olives speared onto gold topped toothpicks.

Standing in the entryway in my ratty sweats, my hair still wet and secured in a wadded mess on top my head with a butterfly clip, the ends of my monkey socks extending by a red inch beyond my toes, a steaming mug of cocoa in my cupped hands; I was overwhelmed with the urge to scratch my ass and belch. Instead I dissolved into a near fit of hysterical laughter and snuggled my face into Julio's silky front before I made things even worse.

As I staggered off to bed moments later I heard Senora stage whisper to her son, in English so I'd be sure and understand.

"Dear. Really. Don't you think she may be carrying this hillbilly thing just a bit too far?"

I woke when Julio slipped into bed beside me—minus those silky pajamas. The moon through the wooden window shutters gilded his body in wide stripes of bluish light. I ran my hands up his sides, watched his face as he moved over me, rose up to meet him flooded with images of pounding tropical rain and light shattered in a steamy jungle canopy. Afterward, with his head still at my breasts, one of his knees drawn up over my hips, I fell back into sleep. I dreamed of dark woods hung with moss the color of old blood, filled with a presence I could neither name or escape. It wasn't fear or dread I felt but the deep surrender of homecoming.

Once I crest the ridge I begin to see bear signs. The wide five-toed prints that look almost like those I make walking barefoot on the beach. Furry, black berry-seeded scat and lots of bear trails. A bear won't detour around much in the woods. It's size lets it go through most every obstacle and this bear has a maze tore through the underbrush, dark shaggy hair marking the trails sides. When I drop down the western side of the ridge and pick up an old deer trail the prints and scat vanish and I relax a little, stop shuffling my feet and singing Patsy Cline at the top of my lungs. Only thing more dangerous than running into a beer when you're alone in the woods is surprising a bear when you're alone in the woods.

It's not yet full daylight when I settle my aching back against the largest Hickory at meadow's edge, slide the bolt on the Winchester and position the rifle across my knees. The only sound is the wind through the high tops of the trees and a ground squirrel scolding softly from a nearby Pine stump. The squirrel pumps his scraggly tail warning me away from his winter treasure of nuts and seeds. If he doesn't settle down soon, I'll have to move or risk this chattering guard warning away the buck.

The meadow is tall brown grass tipped with dry sticky heads this time of year, ringed with brambles and blackberry bushes rich and heavy with fruit just a few weeks ago. Leaning against the tree, my mind filled with last night's love making, I come close to drifting off, decide I'd better stand up, move a bit. Since I'm up I may as well empty my bladder. Rifle slung over my shoulder, chamber full, safety on, I work my way as quietly as possible through the underbrush. A few hundred yards back into the woods, hoping the breeze remains constant keeping my scent downwind of the meadow, I unzip my jeans.

My pants around my ankles, I squat with my bare ass a few inches above the thick humus of the forest floor. At the sound of my pee bouncing off the dying leaves between my spread knees, I rise up a few inches, hold back some so as not to splatter pee on my jeans and underwear. It's another glaring example of God's terrific sense of humor that now, in this awkward half squat with urine steaming onto the frosty ground between my knees, now is when I hear her coming.

I'm sure there are things louder than a bear charging through the woods directly at you while you're squatted with your pants around your ankles. But I can't think of a good example right at this moment. The undergrowth is a tornado of snapping branches as she clears a path for herself. I don't so much stand as levitate, the rifle swinging off my shoulder and rising automatically in my arms to take its position. Some part of my brain knows I'm peeing into my jeans and underwear which are still hobbling me to the spot, but I have a whole other priority going on right at the moment and can't seem to be bothered with ending what my body has already started.

The bear is less than fifty feet from me and she isn't slowing down. On all fours, her massive head swings from left to right with each step. She still doesn't see me or, for the love of God, smell me and I can't think of any way to announce myself to her that isn't going to surprise the living hell out of her. This is definitely the same bear that Uncle Walter and I encountered. Her left shoulder and leg don't quite support her weight. Her gait is awkward and looks painful.

The rifle still at ready I shout, stamp my feet like an idiot, "Get away bear. Don't make me hurt you!"

I'd really like to get my pants off or up. Either way works for me. I can't think of how to do either so I begin shuffling backward, dragging my wet jeans between my legs. I know you're supposed to act confident and assertive if you meet a black bear in the woods. I saw it on the Discovery network. I'm finding it's not all that easy to remain calm and confident with my bare ass hanging in the frosty air and the now full attention of a very startled black bear.

Time for plan B.

I fire a shot over her head.

Bellow at her to "Scat! Run! Get oughta here you stupid bear!"

The shot appears to piss her off. She rises to her full height, looks me right in the eyes and gives me a nice view of that thunderbolt scar along her underarm and chest. Her roar is so much more effective than my own. Whatever urine I have left in my bladder joins the soggy mess between my hiking boots. I'm still shuffling backward while I jack another round into the chamber, still hollering like a mad woman while keeping my best friend tight against my shoulder, sighting down the barrel and praying I don't have to take the shot.

It's not that easy to kill a bear with a bolt action .30-06. They've been known to take a full clip before finally giving up the fight. This one is a lifetime too close for a bad shot to save me and I can't see her disposition improving if I wound her. She drops back down on all fours, swings that big toothy head like a pendulum from hell and keeps coming. We're in a slow ballet her and I. I slide my feet back an inch or two, she moves forward. I shuffle again, shout at her in my best calm assertive voice. She keeps closing the gap, not impressed with my antics. So much for my bear whisperer aspirations.

A person with their wet pants around their ankles can inch backwards with remarkable speed when a threatening bear is closing in on her. But by the time I reach the old hickory where my pack and gear are strewn, the bear has closed the distance. She's no more than twenty feet from me. Way too close. Way, way too close. She rears back up on those tree stump thick hind legs and gives me what I take as my final warning. My last thought before I press the trigger is that I do not want to be found with my bare ass hanging out, half eaten by a bear.

I aim for her heart because a bear's skull is thick enough to deflect a .30-06. I jack in a second round and squeeze off another shot before I realize that her forward motion is not my death but hers. The woods echo with her fall and my screams.

When silence returns to the forest, I walk around the body in a trance, rifle so tight against my shoulder, so much pressure on the trigger guard that, when a hundred years later I accept that the body at my feet is the bear's and not my own, my arm and hand will be numb, no longer a part of my body at all, but an extension of the rifle. The woods seem to exhale as I kneel beside the bear, run my hand over her head, feel joined with this animal forever.

When I finally stand, I fumble in my pocket for my LG Pearl, drop the phone and have to scramble around in the mulch and leaves to find it again. I need to hear Julio's voice, pulling me once again to what our kind calls the real world. Flipped open in my shaking hand the thin phone is black and dead. The shaking arrives in one cold quick wave ending with a small pool of vomited coffee and adrenaline steaming between my feet.

I unbuckle the pack, dig around under the bottled water and insect repellent and granola bars until my hand closes on the two way radio. I flip the switch at the back, depress the wide black button on the side and a reassuring red light blinks at me from the display screen.

"This is Goo Goo Barr. Can y'all hear me down there?"

The static is loud in the morning forest, a rude electronic raspberry cementing the human intrusion that has brought death into these woods.

"Goo Goo?   This is your Aunt Snickers. Is ever thing all right up there?"

"Auntie?   Is Julio there?"

"Unh ah, he hasn't shown up here. Sweetie what's happening?   Did you get that ole buck?"

"No ma'am. I did not. I am just fine but I'm gonna need some help up here."

Uncle Walter's deep voice crackles through the cold air, replacing the softer tones of Aunt Snickers.

"Goo Goo Barr!   What happened up thar?"

"The bear Uncle Walter. She . . . I killed her."

The advantage of a satellite linked two way radio over a cell phone, besides the obvious fact that the cell phone won't work with a mere mountain between it and the transmitting tower, is that a person can release that little black button on the side of the device and folks on the other end can't hear any wailing or choking or hiccupping that may or may not be gong on.

Jehovah God's voice thundering from the heavens, blasting his chosen people with scorching love, must have been more powerful and demanding, but Uncle Walter bellowing through the scratch and shriek of that radio, 'what in the name of sam hill is goin' on up there?', that's as close as I ever need to get to the voice of an all powerful and all protective God.

Once Uncle knows I'm not hurt, just shook up in what he has the audacity to call my 'natural girlie way', he assures me he'll be up in a few hours with Uncles Neil and

Earl to help me pack the bear down the mountain. I tell him I'll have her skinned out and start on the butchering and maybe we'll make it down the mountain by nightfall. Then I ask him to bring Julio with him.

He depresses his little side button so I hear the drawn out sigh of exasperation, before he answers me.

"Sweetheart, I know you love that—that feller, but Honey he's gonna be worthless as tits on a boar hawg at butchering and hauling that bear home."

I hold down that send button. "I want him here with me Uncle Walter. I need him here with me. Bring him."

As I set the walkie talkie on top the pack and get ready to start skinning I have two clear thoughts. First, in all the world the person I most want at this moment is Julio. It is true that, as Uncle Walter pointed out, he has no hunting or hiking expertise, yet it is Julio who I most need right now. I hold my left hand out in front of me, stare at my future. For the first time, there is no hesitation, no confusion. I center the ring on my finger, accept my future role as the wife of Julio Monterey.

Secondly, while I know for a fact that I have calmed down a good bit and, cool and competent hunter that I am, have just about recovered from the excitement of The Great Bear Kill, nonetheless, the reason my ass is near about frozen appears to be because I am still standing with it waving in the frosty air with my soggy pants around my ankles.

Using hickory branches and a rope and pulley system that convince me I missed my calling as a structural engineer, I manage to turn the bear over onto her back. My plan is to make a ventral incision just below the heart working my way to the tail and then cutting laterally to the inside of all four legs. A bear skin rug in front of the rock fireplace at what will be Julio and my home, that's what I am imagining.

Not that there has ever been any danger of Julio becoming the kind of husband inclined to boss me around, but still, the skin of a bear I've killed and skinned myself isn't a bad reminder to husband and future children of the true nature of the redneck goddess who will be ruling the house. Maybe I'll get my picture taken arranged elegantly along its length in champagne toned silk pajamas; a thoughtful Christmas present for The Sainted Mother.

It's coming up on noon by the time I have the front of the bear skinned out. My first bullet went directly into her heart, which was a lucky shot for me at the time, but a bloody mess to deal with now. The second shot must have hit as she was already falling forward because it entered at the base of her neck, went up the back of her throat and into her brain. Working like this, making the decisions that always come with skinning an animal whose hide I want to preserve, settles me down.

It's a shock how quickly the spirit and soul of a living breathing creature moves into the next realm leaving just fur and meat and blood and innards. Pretty well covered in a good deal of this bear's earthly remains, I'm contemplating on how this beautiful she-bear and my moment of communion in that split second between life and death is preserved intact, untouched, as is the eternal spirit of the animal herself. This here, this work I'm doing with a knife, this is just a bloody mess of butchering.

I'm shaky with effort and the aftereffects of the rush of the adrenalin spiked kill as I separate the head intact from the front down to the skin on the back of the neck. I don't have the tools with me to do a good job with the delicate cutting around the eyes and nose. That'll have to wait until I get the hide back down the mountain.

One of those granola bars I have in my pack might help with my shaking, but given the amount of blood and fur I have smeared on my hands and face and clothes, I elect to first roll the body back onto its front so I can finish the skinning. I do smear blood around in the pack pulling out a quart of water which I open and drink down in one glorious pull. Then I use my latent engineering skills once more, roll the carcass gently onto its front and finish the skinning. I cut the paws off at the first leg joint, the pads being another tricky skinning job that will have to wait until I get to Uncle Nuggie's and resurrect my taxidermy knives.

When I finally have the skin rolled with the head and paws wrapped around the bundle like some macabre sleeping bag at a slumber party for the deranged, I take a rest. Sinking down with my back against the brindled bark of the Hickory, I peel the wrapper from a granola bar, ignore the blood and black hair coating my hands, and eat the thing in two big bites. Uncles Walter, Earl and Neil along with my sweet Julio are on their way. They're driving ATV's around through Preston's Yate's development as far as the ridge. Last report over the radio was that they are walking up the front of Martin's Ridge and will be here in about an hour.

Uncle Walter also reported that a 'potful of other folks who got no business getting themselves involved are coming your way though why in tarnation they think they need to do so is a mystery.'

By which I assume he means the aunts are hitching a ride on the ATVs. Both Auntie Ruth and Snickers are more than capable of keeping pace with the Uncles on a hike, so, despite Uncle's disapproval, I'm not worried about the extra company on the hike back home.

I have devoured the second granola bar and am digging around in the pack looking for the third one I know I put in there this morning when I hear something crashing through the underbrush coming from the same direction as the she bear whose skin is now rolled beside me and whose skinned body now lies exposed on the blood encrusted forest floor.

An overwhelming sense of déjà-vu roots me to the ground, causes my tired brain to flash back so completely to the earlier events of the day that my first clear image of the actual moment is the smell of hot urine once again wetting my already ruined underwear and jeans. I hear a shell being jacked into the chamber of the .30-06 before I realize I'm standing with the rifle once again tight against my shoulder, my thumb sliding the safety off, the trigger guard cold under my finger. The bear is moving on all fours, its head high and jerking awkwardly up and down as it sniffs the air for traces of its mother. Seventy five pounds or so, the orphaned cub comes directly to what's left of its mother's scent--me and the rolled skin at my side.

Chapter Seventeen ★

I drop a folded bill into the long handled wicker basket and notice a thin line of dried blood along the cuticle of my right thumb. Pastor Coleman implores that we 'be filled with a generosity of the spirit worthy of your people oh Lord,' as I rub my index finger along my thumb nail and meditate on just how difficult it is to wash away the blood of a kill.

It wasn't my aunties who showed up at the meadow with the uncles and Julio. It was Cassandra Hollywood and her crew. They found me lying under the hickory having fallen into an exhausted sleep, the she-bear's hide and the baby bear cradled in the curve of my body. I'm sure you've seen the pictures. They were on the nightly news here in Georgia and are already making the rounds of the internet.

I look savage. My hair is a curly flame red aura of death around my blood streaked face. I'm sure it was the camera angle, but I appear to have more black bear hair stuck to my face than the cub's natural mother. The young bear is sleeping with its head in the hollow of my neck, one front paw on my shoulder, the other resting on the bridge of its mother's lifeless nose. The only face in the picture with its eyes open, the she-bear appears to be staring directly at the camera.

By the time the rescue party and I hiked to the ATVs waiting at the ridge, the stars were ice blue gems set in an indigo canopy, the air biting cold. The uncles and Julio packed the skin and what they could of the bear meat and the rest we left as an offering to the ravens and other scavengers. I walked point, the snuffling cub at my heels.

This morning the cub is in the same old section of the barn where I've kept strays since I was big enough to carry home a baby porcupine entangled in barbed wire, drag a pregnant cat out from the berry briars, or rescue a cottontail from the drooling mouth of General Lee. Julio and I drove over before church and I fed the little guy on the goat's milk I've used to nurse animals since Uncle Walter took to keeping a half dozen or so of the brush eating critters out behind the chicken pen. The cub bleated in recognition when he saw me, even though I'm pretty sure I smelled more like gardenia bath scrub than his mama. I'm doing my best not to get attached to the little orphan. Phineas Martin is coming this afternoon to carry the poor thing to a five thousand acre bear sanctuary on the northern slope of the Smokies.

Phin, for whom I babysat each and every day of his fourth summer, was in his official capacity as county game warden when he appeared at our front door as I was sipping from my second cup of coffee. With apologies and a good bit of hitching up of his pants and fumbling with the clip board he clutched in his sweaty hand, he explained that, since I did not have a bear tag or license, I was gonna be ree-quired to write up a report in triplicate explaining to the great state of Georgia just exactly what had happened up that mountain.

"Well, hell Phin, I shot the poor thing so she wouldn't eat me. There ain't that much to tell."

"Just be grateful we ain't in California Miss Barr. We'd be having this here conversation in a jail cell."

We stand to join the choir in singing *Just as I Am*. Senora Monterey, on the other side of Julio, holds the red hymnal in both well manicured hands and sings clearly in a sweet soprano. She appears to have recovered from the bloody homecomings of the Redneck Goddesses last night. When Julio left with the Uncles, his mother joined my Aunties at contest headquarters in the new Bessie Smith Park. In retrospect she may not have been quite ready for this induction into the tribal customs of South Georgia's indigenous folk.

By the time our group made its appearance, the city woman had already witnessed the return to headquarters of thirteen young contestants. All were coated in mud and dirt, most were also smeared with at least a small portion of the blood of whatever unfortunate fish or animal they had dragged back from the woods or plucked from the murk of the local waters. The Burnett twins had a string of catfish to impress even Uncle's Earl and Neil. Lizzie Ragsdale got her buck, a forked horn, though it didn't weigh as much as the cub I orphaned. Lizzie pulled it off the front of the jeep and posed with the animal draped around her neck like some Kafka inspired shawl. I've seen the pictures. The woman looks like the Huntress Diana incarnate. Or a serial killer. Depending on one's orientation.

All told three deer, forty three fish, six rabbits, eight squirrel, an opossum, two armadillo and a nice assortment of mushrooms, herbs and wild flowers met their end to satisfy the requirements of contest. The judges, three of the six not being from around here, appeared equally impressed and horrified. Senora Monterey, a woman who routinely deals with grid locked traffic, third world police and sit down dinners for ambassadors, was shaken. Hell, Aunts Ruth and Snickers were a little shaken. This was not precisely the image they had in mind when this whole Preston Yates extravaganza began. Cassandra had enough footage of blood drenched hillbillies to make several powerful documentaries. The only thing missing was Michael Moore.

So, when our little group rolled in before midnight with just under three hundred pounds of hacked meat, a grinning bear head, and a baby bear who took instant fright at the lights, climbed me like a tree trunk and draped itself over my face, well, Senora had dealt with pretty much all she could handle. Aunt Ruth drove the trembling woman to her and Collin's house and put her to bed on the linen sheets of her guest room.

It is my understanding that the only truly dangerous moment of the evening came when Senora, who at that point was helping with the record keeping, had suggested, under her breath and in Spanish, that Lizzie Ragsdale needed to go home and clean herself up. Lizzie was restrained by her grinning cousin Johnny who pointed out to her that *ducha* is the Spanish word for shower and Senora was recommending simply a little soapy water applied to the outside of her bloody body.

Uncle Nuggie was there when we straggled into the park. He had thirty pounds of salt and a promise that he'd finish skinning the bear's head and paws and tan the hide for me. I didn't argue. By then I was sleepwalking. Not that easy to do with a seventy five pound frightened baby with three inch claws attached to your head and chest. For once in my life I was delighted to have someone else take control. I let Uncle Walter crate the crying cub and Julio lead me to the flame jobbed jeep.

Once home Julio undressed us both. I stood shaky legged and trembling under a hot shower while he washed my hair and his, soaped me down until the water no longer ran rust colored into the drain at our feet. Then, while I sat on the closed toilet seat wrapped in a thick white towel, he cleaned the tub and filled it with steamy gardenia scented water. There was a moment, stretched full length in the near scalding water, when every muscle seemed to loosen and I entered a world of swirling mists and spirit bears.

I awoke at dawn to the smell of coffee and the lilting voice of Aunt Ruth blending with Julio's deeper tones coming from the kitchen. Lifting my head off the pillow and swinging my feet to the braided bedside rug, I was reminded that I'd been marked with the desperation of the cub. Examining myself in the bathroom mirror, I claimed the stripes and bruises as restitution for the killing of his mother. It had been her life or mine, but it was me who encroached into her shrinking territory. I figure I got off cheap with a few scars.

Bessie Smith Park is already filling with people by the time Julio, his mother, Uncle Walter and I pull into the gravel parking lot at just after noon. The contestants have gotten themselves up and attended early morning services at their church of choice. Having broken the contest rules by calling for help, I informed Aunt Ruth this morning when I limped into the kitchen that I was removing myself from the contest. She took one look at the gouges on my forehead and cheeks, the interesting new way I had of walking by swinging one leg forward in a mini arch to avoid moving my left hip which sported a bruise the size of dinner plate, all topped by hair which had dried against my pillow and now formed an elaborate gnarled wedge around my face, and her exact words were, 'Perhaps that would be best Dear.'

Relieved of the responsibility of aspiring Goddesshood, I hugged Aunt Ruth goodbye and told her I'd see her at the contest. Julio and I enjoyed nearly two hours of cuddling before Phineas, in his new persona as official government representative, showed up at our door and jump started our official day. It was then that we swung by Uncle Walters for my morning visit with the cub. Julio drove to pick up his mother while I did my best with a roll of scotch tape I got from Uncle Walter's junk drawer to remove bear hair and slobber from Aunt Snickers loaner dress. We met up again with Uncle Walter minutes before the choir called us inside with *Bringing in the Sheaves* and arranged ourselves in the Barr pew at the Sluggard's Service of Jesus the Redeemer Babtist church on Lee Ave.

My borrowed clothes are an attempt to redeem myself in the eyes of my future mother-in-law. I'm wearing a proper, calf-length wool blend dress, deep burgundy with navy trim and short heels, with panty hose no less, topped with a navy blue, good republican cloth coat. I've even corralled my hair into what I delude myself into believing is an elegant braid but may more closely resembled a frayed and flaming rope. My main goal for today though, in the hope of working my way into the good graces of Senora Monterey, is to avoid all contact with blood, butchering, knives or anything else that might further cement her image of me as an uncultured barbarian unfit to raise her future grandchildren.

Two long tables are set up under a red, white and blue striped canvas pavilion whose sides flap gently in the breeze wafting the lard rich smells of good home cooking. Standing behind the tables, all in identical pink bibbed aprons are the remaining Redneck Goddess contestants. The Burnett twins appear to be naked under those hideous aprons, but a closer look reveals gold tube tops and low rider short shorts. I grin, knowing the Aunties foolishly planned for the knee length, boob covering aprons to tone down the sex appeal at this last event. Aunt Ruth and Aunt Snickers, of all people, should have known that you can put a country girl in a gunny sack and her true nature is still gonna shine through and starch the trousers of every male within stick throwing distance.

We've missed the part of the contest where the judges did their best to appear official while dribbling grease on their chins. Those five red faced men and one harassed looking woman are now gathered under the gazebo, apparently tallying scores and doing their Goddess making. The Burnett twins are frying catfish and serving them up with hush puppies, cold slaw and sweet tea. With Senora Monterey and Uncle Walter between us, Julio and I stroll the lengths of the tables, sampling Lizzie's venison potpie, and Loralee Sinclair's rabbit enhanced Brunswick Stew. The Foster twins missed their buck but returned with enough wild oyster mushrooms to stir in with a few of their mama's hens and make a delicious dish they're calling Buck Fever Casserole.

The day is sunny and brisk, the breeze just strong enough to carry the green, tangy smell of the nearby creek and piney woods. Families visit with kin and neighbors, children chase each other along the outskirts of the crowd. Somebody has cranked up Waylon and Johnny out under the magnolias and a melody of trains and broken hearts carries softly across the park. Senora Monterey appears to be relaxing into the moment, enjoying herself as she picks at her Brunswick Stew while Julio does his best to describe for her the joys of grits and biscuits and cornbread. All is going well.

Until we reach the small crafts market next to the pavilion. The four of us are sharing a bag of boiled peanuts as we work our way past pine needle baskets, the inevitable veneer dulcimers and beeswax candles, homemade fudge and elaborately dressed porcelain dolls. It's the look on the face of Senora Monterey that draws my eyes up.

I'm staring at my own sleeping face. Big as life, smeared with blood and short black hairs and twice the size of the bear's head resting in my elbow.

"It's my best seller by far," Cassandra tells me sweetly from behind her plywood booth. The poster has a price tag of $9.99.

My first thought is that this is why one should never allow strangers with cameras into a family gathering. My second is that, even in heels, pantyhose and an elegant dress, I can clear that plywood stand and take this bitch out in 2.5 seconds.

Senora Monterey rests her hand on my arm, soft as a butterfly, forbidding as a weaving cobra.

"Darling," she says to Julio in soft Spanish as she juts her chin toward the poster, "this will be your wife?"

When Julio grins at her and kisses the top of his mother's head, she shrugs and says something which I choose to translate as 'so be it,' though, 'it's your funeral' may be closer to correct.

To the clueless Cassandra, Senora scolds, "You young lady, you must take care that your ambition does not lead you into the same fate as the bear."

With that The Sainted Mother puts her arms through Julio and mine and, gently, ever so firmly, leads us away from the potential killing zone, a bemused Uncle Walter bringing up the rear.

No one really doubts the outcome of the contest. Loralee Sinclair smiles sweetly as she accepts third place. The clapping of the Auntie's clearly marking her as their favorite. Lizzie Ragsdale is less gracious about accepting second place. When the shared first place is announced the Burnett twins jump, squeal, hug each other, do a little hippity hop hop across the stage that ends with a bouncy victory dance that threatens to expose more than the joy of winning. The Aunties, worn to a frazzle and without hope of redeeming the debacle, simply watch from the sidelines. The crowd whistles and stomps its approval as the twins hug the necks of each and every judge before taking up their positions on each side of the draped statue.

I have explained the Bessie Smith Legend to Senora Monterey.

"So this woman, the one who poisoned the northern soldiers, this Bessie Smith, she did not exist?" she asked as she sipped sweet tea.

"Oh," I tried once again to explain. "She exists. It's just that here, in the south, stories don't have to have actually happened to be true."

To which the woman had shrugged her shoulders and said only, "It is the same everywhere."

Now the Jefferson Davis High School band makes a rough start into The Bonnie Blue Flag, recovers with the entrance of the tuba just as the newly crowned Redneck Goddesses each pull a braided red silk rope attached to either side of the drape. Gladys's side comes up faster, she overcorrects to wait for Gloria, they both dissolve into giggles and the band hiccups along, hoping to make up in volume what they lack in execution. Finally the twins recover themselves, wiggle their hind ends, bounce their boobies and, in unison, reveal the statue while the artist, the grinning Kristen Yates, looks on from the sidelines.

The only sound is the band stumbling its way through Dixie.

The statue is bronze, clumsily executed with the flowing lines and correct proportions of a good, if twisted, copy of the original marble. Bessie Smith, attired in a voluminous skirted pioneer dress complete with bonnet and high topped shoes is a third again as large as the second figure. Across her lap, his vulnerable throat exposed as his head lolls lifelessly against her arm, lies a fallen soldier, his cap and tattered uniform marking him as Confederate. Bessie's face, nearly hidden behind the bonnet, looks down in anguish on this brave Rebel lad.

That there is no rebel soldier in the Bessie Smith story is the least of the problems with this tribute designed and executed by Kristen Yates. If Andy Warhol and Jeff Foxworthy got together after seeing The Pieta on a trip to Italy, well, this here might be what they'd design.

I can see the aunties from where I stand. They appear dumbstruck. The band winds down. The echo of the last cymbal and trombone sinks into the silence.

From behind me, the sound of a beer can being crushed against what I can only surmise is a forehead brings us all back to the moment. It's Uncle Earl that starts the commotion.

"The way I heard it, that there is pretty near exact what ole Bessie looked like."

Uncle Neil leads the crowd in an awe inspired rebel yell and sums it up with the proclamation that, "It's like that there little sculptor gal was working from an actual photograph, ain't it?"

I cannot shake from my head an image of Michelangelo sitting beside his white haired God, tearful face buried in his gnarled hands, begging the Good Lord to explain again why he saw fit to create Rednecks.

Julio leans across his mother, grins wickedly at me, winks and raises one eyebrow, "Is *absolutemente perfecto*, no?"

I look at the good folks around me, nearly all of whom wear grins of recognition on their faces. I breath deep of the crisp, afternoon air, sharp with the smells of fried food, piney woods and the precise mix of home that makes up the red dirt under my feet. My smile is wide and bone deep as I wink back and concur.

Yep. Absolutely perfect.

Pamela Foster, a Pacific Northwest redneck, married a man from Georgia and fell in love with most all things southern. When she and her husband retired to a tin roofed house in the rainforest of Spanish speaking Panama, the author craved the sound and nuances of her native English. Visited by many of her husband's southern friends and relatives, she came to adore the drawled version of the language.

Redneck Goddess is proof of her adoration for both Latin America and the American South.

Currently living with her husband and his service dog, Chesty, in Fayetteville, Arkansas, she is a member of the Northwest Arkansas Writers Workshop, Ozarks Writers League, and the Oklahoma Writers Federation. She is currently working on a novel, *Bigfoot Blues*, set in her hometown of Eureka, California.

You can visit Pamela at these addresses:
pamelafoster2011@gmail.com
http://pamelafoster.blogspot.com
www.authorpamelafoster.com